FOREWORD

Welcome to 'Crazy Creatures – Fiendish Fiction'.

For our Young Writers autumn competition we invited Key Stage 2 pupils to write a saga inspired by a crazy creature. These creatures could be a mythical beast that just walked out a fantasy world, it could be an alien from outer space, it could be a creature from the darkest jungle or it could even be your household pet. Whichever creature had your imagination running wild we wanted to hear about it!

The challenge was tricky; pupils had to not only create a creature and a story around their creature they had to do it all in under 100 words! The pupils rose magnificently to the challenge and the stories we received were fantastic. As always the stories were of a very high standard, they were well written, engaging and humorous so I would like to congratulate everyone whose work has been included in this publication. I hope this competition has inspired you to keep writing and that I look forward to reading more of your work in our future competitions!

Emily Wilson

CONTENTS

Matthew Riddell-Dillet (9)	54		Zak Mclaren (10)	94
Finn Verhoeven (9)	55		Aran Hay (10)	95
Zuzu Rose Kennedy Johnston (9)	56		Robbie Ferguson (10)	96
Blair Gallagher (9)	57		Eve Falconer (10)	97
Adam Kennedy (9)	58		Owen Morrison (10)	98
Cameron Fensom (9)	59		Zuzia Karusewicz (10)	99
Grace McCaig (9)	60		Ciara Morris (9)	100
Aadam Hussain (9)	61		Niamh Jack (9)	101
Ian Menzies (9)	62		Ava Laing (9)	102
April Methven (9)	63		Cerys Brett (9)	103
India Stevens (9)	64		Helen Latta (9)	104
Emma Jane Wallace (9)	65		Michael Glanville (9)	105
Zac Taylor (9)	66			

Matthew Riddell-Dillet (9) 54 — first column data continues:

Zac Taylor (9) 66
Ava Taylor (9) 67
George Livingstone Irvine (9) 68
Monty Smith (9) 69
Aaryn Mckenna (9) 70
Hamish Ferguson (9) 71
Elena Beverland (9) 72
Victoria Cara Murphy (9) 73
Oscar Parkins (8) 74
Xavier Ndoumbe (9) 75
Bobby Shearer (9) 76
Callum Robinson (9) 77
Rosie Grace Everington (9) 78
Adam Howat (9) 79
Fin Patchett (9) 80
Marley Haston (9) 81
Louis Di Mascio (9) 82

Georgetown School, Dumfries

Mirryn Fergusson (9) 106
Ryan William Rodgers (9) 107
Amy Johnston (9) 108
Clara Elizabeth Conchar (9) 109
Joe Alison (8) 110
Aiden Stewart Mcculloch (9) 111
Evan Robertson (9) 112
Katie Aitchison (8) 113
Jack Trosh (9) 114
Junior Pinnock (9) 115
Fahad Gazi (9) 116
Caethon Mutch (9) 117
Morven Kirk (8) 118
Billy Gray (8) 119

Echline Primary School, South Queensferry

Grace Simm (10) 83
Issy Wood (9) 84
Ella Kirsty Balanowski (10) 85
Eva Blair (10) 86
Elliot Murphy (10) 87
Emily Simm (10) 88
James Yule (10) 89
Luke Collins (10) 90
James Mills (10) 91
Tegan MacPherson (10) 92
Freya Ridgway (10) 93

Lincluden School, Dumfries

Leigh Kirkpatrick (8) 120
Ethan Mcnaught (9) 121
Kieran Carruthers (8) 122
Cassie Mcgregor (9) 123
Eilidh White (9) 124
Kendra Bobbi Douglas (9) 125
Mikey Warner (9) 126
Kaidy Tanbini (8) 127

Lochside School, Dumfries

Lauren Fleming (11)	128
Tyler Wilson (11)	129
Destinee Xiomara Houston (11)	130
Elise Bell (10)	131
Logan Byers (11)	132
Isla Talor Hammond (12)	133
Deryn Kathryn Wylie (11)	134

Pencaitland Primary School, Tranent

Eleanor Hemsley (9)	135
Noah Ellis Macdonald (9)	136
Ruby Mosses-Hoy (9)	137
Zara Ashaye (9)	138
Niamh McLean (9)	139
Rosie Graham (9)	140
Iona McLean (9)	141
Lucy Elizabeth McMillan (9)	142
Molly Budgen (9)	143
Niamh Cadzow (9)	144
Duncan McWilliam-Snow (9)	145
Elliot Smith	146
Kayleigh Brunton (9)	147
Josh Noble (10)	148
Ollie Armstrong (9)	149

Pumpherston And Uphall Station Community Primary School, Livingston

Julia Zuziak (11)	150
Rory Mclean (11)	151
Craig Cantley (11)	152
Paigh-Florence Dearie (11)	153
Donatella Fargnoli (11)	154
Kadan Brennan (11)	155
Hayden Carroll (11)	156
Lydia Purves (11)	157
Jack Redmond (11)	158
Louisa Black (11)	159
Lewis Patterson (11)	160

Jack Ryan Taylor Hamilton (11)	161
Matthew Rutherford (11)	162
Hannah Anderson (11)	163
Shannon Vermeulen (11)	164
Ella Rachel Watson (11)	165
Lewis Campbell (10)	166
Sophie Campbell (11)	167
Kimber Shearer (11)	168
Samantha Price (11)	169
Sophie Martin (11)	170
Cameron Brydon (11)	171
Aaron John Cleland (11)	172
Katie Martin (11)	173

Ranworth Square Primary School, Liverpool

Sophie Elizabeth Childs (10)	174
Sophia Shaw (7)	175
Ella Dambis (10)	176
Samuel Scott Mercer (8)	177
Lexi McGreevy (10)	178
Adam Dean (11)	179
Harry McMahon (10)	180
Ellen McNulty (10)	181
Taighlor Rogerson (10)	182
Leah Sephton (8)	183
Nathan Boyle (7)	184
Luke Lawless (7)	185

St Alban's Catholic Primary School, Wallasey

Max Marnell (8)	186
Ebony Michelle Johnstone (8)	187
Marco Clenkian (8)	188
Ellie Toner (8)	189
Chloe Mary Kathleen Hammond (8)	190
Ozz Kindred (9)	191
Reuben Spivey (7)	192
Eva Easdown (8)	193
Alfie John Feeney (8)	194
Chloe Ashley Blyth (7)	195

Libby Hamilton (9)	196	Mia Morrison (10)	233
Eleanor Claire Cronin (8)	197	Imran Mohammad Zafar (10)	234
Harry Jonathan Smith (8)	198	Finlay McWilliam	235
Sam Funcks (8)	199	Danny Lewis	236
Harry Marshall-Hose (8)	200	Himmat Singh	237
Sophie Baker (8)	201	Motiya Muzzamil (10)	238
Woody Clewlow (8)	202	Freya Auchincloss	239
Ashton Traynor (8)	203	James Craig (10)	240
Amy Goodwill (8)	204	Emily McKenzie	241
Reuben Swaine (8)	205	Fred Davis	242
Orla Maguire (8)	206	Beth Adams	243
Isobel Prescott (9)	207	India Faith Young (10)	244
Sadie Pearson (9)	208	Lewis Johnston	245
Rio Emerick Grant (8)	209	Sean Brannen	246
Lucy Louise Donegan-Bowen (8)	210	Liam Murray (10)	247
Sammy Michael Sheldon (7)	211		

St Saviour's Catholic Primary School, Ellesmere Port

Christopher James Mannings (8)	212
Chloe Louise Williams (9)	213
Romilly Carol McKinnon (8)	214
Finley Connor (9)	215
Kaitlyn Olivia Lomas (8)	216
Joel Henri-Reid (8)	217
Luke George Howells (8)	218
Oliver Timson (8)	219
Joseph Hesketh (8)	220
Charlotte McNeill-Williams (8)	221
Mai Allen-Coates (8)	222
Gracie Bird (7)	223
Adam Williamson (8)	224
John James Howard (9)	225
Charlie Curtis (8)	226

Noah Jackson (8)	248
Clancy Lillia Oldam (7)	249
Amber-Alexis MacDonald (7)	250
Katie Jones (7)	251

St Helens PACE, St. Helens

Maddison Grayson (9)	227
Larissa Wood (10)	228
Emilie Kelly (7)	229
Sharyn Billingsley (7)	230
McKenzie Briers (7)	231

St John's Primary School, Edinburgh

Tara Divito (10)	232

THE STORIES

Bomb Saves The Day

It was a cheery day when suddenly people started to run and scream, 'Argh!'

The mega bomb had been stolen by someone! It must be found, so Bomb ran to the mayor and asked if he could go on a quest to find the mega bomb. The mayor said yes and provided him with supplies and he was on his way.

He reached the rainforest of monsters, and a monster with vibes and mega sharp teeth caught Bomb.

'Ha-ya!' Another monster cut the monster off Bomb, then together they found the mega bomb and the city was saved.

Bethany Kerr (9)

The Lucky Paintbrush

Paint Star has got a star body and devil ears.
One day, Paint Star was just painting like normal.
He turned away to get some more paint and when
he turned back he screamed, 'Where's my lucky
paintbrush?'
He went to go and see if his paintbrush was in the
woods. After two hours of looking he said, 'Maybe
it is with the pallet again,' with a tear in his eye.
So he walked back and saw something shimmer in
the sun. He walked towards it and screamed,
'There's my lucky paintbrush!'

Grace Higgins (9)

Munchie Monster

The Munchie Monster lives in our school. He has spiky hair, big grabby hands and ten googly eyes which he uses to find food. He likes to eat new HB pencils and big white rubbers.
One day the teacher screamed, 'Where are my pencils and rubbers?'
The children sniggered and said, 'It is the Munchie Monster!' But she did not believe them. So she went to her drawer and she saw the Munchie Monster! She screamed and grabbed him then she threw him on the floor. Muchie Monster was sick and he spat the HB pencils and rubbers out!

Sophie Nelson (11)
Beattock Primary School, Moffat

Crazy Creatures Mini Saga

Googly-Eyed Gook is a lone predator who doesn't need any help. He has two lives - this one and one where he turns into school classroom objects. He enjoys both of them, but there's one problem - he does the predator hunting life more than the school one, and he only wants to do one now. He is confused and having a hard time.
He finally decides and he picks... the school one!
He is so happy about his decision and he is more confident that the decision he made was the right one.
Everyone loves him now.

Tobey John Fullerton (11)
Beattock Primary School, Moffat

Super Small

There was a super small guy who stole sweets from people's pockets. He lived in the pockets of kids and the police just couldn't catch him. He would hide in trash cans and drains, and even in dogs' fur. He stole over 500,000,000 sweets in a year. He ate all the sweets he stole in a week! He became a very ill and fat little person, but he stopped stealing sweets because he was too fat to fit in people's pockets!

Bellamy Anderson (11)
Beattock Primary School, Moffat

Tornado Monster

The Tornado Monster sneaks around the streets like a spy looking for people to save or baddies to stop. He also has an underground base. Tornado Monster can shoot out tornados that are black, red, light blue, dark blue and dark green.
One day, he saw a guy stealing a woman's handbag, so Tornado Monster shot out tornados at him and got back the woman's handbag. The thief was last seen cleaning windows!

Kiera Minto (9)
Beattock Primary School, Moffat

Creepy Runner

Creepy Runner is a creature who lives in flowers. He has two horns and two wiggly legs. When people smell the flowers, he runs up their nose and makes them sneeze!
One day, Creepy Runner felt lonely, so he decided to run up someone's nose, but he got caught in their bogeys because they didn't sneeze. When they did finally sneeze, he landed on another flower and then he found his brother!

Bethany Anderson (8)
Beattock Primary School, Moffat

Wing Loss

Spiky is a mini monster but can be really fierce.
One day Spiky was in the town, but nobody saw
him because he was flying. But suddenly, a seagull
bumped into him and he lost a wing. Spiky fell and
landed on a bouncy castle and his spikes burst it,
and the kids all landed on their bottoms! So Spiky
ran off.
He saw a toy shop which had toy wings and then
he could fly again!

Caelan McAleese (7)
Beattock Primary School, Moffat

Fasty McFast Car And His Exhaust

One day, Fasty McFast Car was zooming down the street. Because he went too fast, there was smoke coming out of his exhaust. Then all the cars were crashing into each other and he felt bad. So he went to the garage and inside he got his exhaust fixed.

Now he goes slowly and carefully and his name is Slowy McSlow Car. He is now a rescue car too.

Brandon Peter Hughes (9)
Beattock Primary School, Moffat

Hagnoo's Escape

'Good morning world,' said Hagnoo. 'Let's go to the Gooie Looie river, where I think I'll have a nap.'
'Ha,' said Fangnang, 'let's steal Hagnoo!'
Soon, Hagnoo woke up. 'Where am I? This isn't the gooie looie river!'
'Ha, you fool, you are in a container, now let me drive my space rocket!'
'I'm so bored... wait, maybe I can turn invisible so Fangnang can't see me. Okay, here we go.'
'Huh? Where is Hagnoo? I'm going to open the container...'
'...Yes! I'm free, now I can fly home, away from Fangnang.'
Later... 'Phew, I think I'll have a nap!'

Chloe McElroy (8)
Bridgend Primary School, Linlithgow

The Monster Fight

One dark night, Spotty Spark the monster was scaring a little girl, but he heard a creak on the floor. He slowly turned around and saw a puppy! He screamed and took a portal to Planet Fire, only to find Rain Fire waiting for him. Rain Fire is Spotty Spark's worst enemy. Spotty Spark said, 'What are you doing here?'
Rain Fire said, 'To fight you, that's why!'
Spotty Spark said, 'Okay, prepare to lose!'
They had an epic battle and Spotty Spark won.
Rain Fire said, 'Okay, can we be friends now?'
Spotty Spark replied, 'Of course!'

Gemma Andi McGill (7)
Bridgend Primary School, Linlithgow

The Lots Of Eyes Monster

Once upon a time there was a monster called Tricky, he was my enemy.

I was going for a walk in the woods, but Tricky came, so I sat down. He came up to me and I said, 'Go away! You know I don't like you.'

So he said, 'Fight me!'

I said, 'Fine, I will win.' So I punched, kicked, pushed and slapped him. 'You will learn not to come here again, and don't ask to fight with me again!'

He went home and so did I, then I went to see the other monsters to tell them.

Lucy Sutherland (8)
Bridgend Primary School, Linlithgow

Bloodshed's Adventure

Bloodshed woke up on is home planet and met Jim and Jake, then they all got into a fight. Bloodshed got knocked out.

He woke up on a spaceship and noticed he could shape-shift. 'So weird,' he said to himself. Then he heard footsteps coming closer to the door and the door opened slowly... They saw him and said hello. Then Bloodshed said hello to the person.

The person took Bloodshed to the 'memoriser' room to help him remember what had happened. Would Bloodshed remember...?

Cayden James Chalmers (8)
Bridgend Primary School, Linlithgow

Monster Vs Rebels

A long time ago, in a galaxy far, far away, there was a monster flying in space and he landed on a mysterious planet. It was a rebel planet. He found out it was a rebel planet because it had a base. The rebels were spying on him. Luckily, he found out and he destroyed them. The rebel leader came with millions of soldiers, but luckily the monster had some robots to help him. The rebels were destroyed again, except for the leader, but they all lost their powers.
The monster and the robots won!

Jack Rafferty (9)

Bridgend Primary School, Linlithgow

The Fluffy, Spotty Monster

One day, there was a monster called Tricky. He heard a sound that he didn't know. Suddenly, the monster went outside and there was a robot. The robot took Tricky to a spaceship, but when they got in it they saw something scary, like a monster coming to get them. But it was only a shadow. Then the robot said, 'Can I come to your house?' 'Yes,' said Tricky.

So they went back home and went to bed, and in the morning they went to the beach.

Liam Long (8)
Bridgend Primary School, Linlithgow

Scattered Ending

Frostburst was eating his lunch with Frankey. Frostburst was sitting down retracing his ice spikes on his hands. Frankey was a shape-shifter bird who was blue.

Suddenly, there was the noise of crunching ice, so Frostburst looked over a rock. Black Elves were coming. The elves said, 'Frostburst, we're going to get you!'

'Frankey!' shouted Frostburst, backflipping over a rock and pushing his spikes out.

Then he spotted something that could end his life! Millions of armoured ice creatures were marching from the south with swords, shields, spears, bows and arrows. There were water creatures with them too...

Alexander Clark (10)
Cargilfield School, Edinburgh

Don't Lose Control

'Aargghh!'

Crash!

'I... I can still talk, uh,' Fluff-Scream mumbled. 'But where am I?'

She had just gone for a fly around the parking lot when she went out of control and flew into a lamp post and thumped to the ground.

Fluff-Scream was a wolf, but she had fairy-like wings. She wore a red dress and a blue bow.

Whoosh! A gigantic blob on wheels hurtled by.

'Argh!' she screamed for the second time. Then came a voice she knew all too well: 'Ahh, so we meet again, your piercing scream gave the game away!'

It was Buster...

Amelia Wordie (10)
Cargilfield School, Edinburgh

Guppy The Furry Beast

Guppy hid in the darkness. Loud bangs came from outside. He stuck out one eye and saw that his beloved family had died because of Bubblechops. He squeezed into the corner and cried from his five eyes. His diamond tooth became dull and fell out. Some hours later he woke up, his furry body damp with tears. He flew out and flew around, wailing miserably. The great cliffs were lonely without his friends. His tiny belly gurgled so he dived into the sea for fish.

Suddenly, a dark shape loomed up. 'Oh no,' Guppy whispered.

It was the dreaded Bubblechops...

Fergus Pim (10)
Cargilfield School, Edinburgh

The Magic Sweet

Queeny Sweet Pop came from a land far, far away called Sugar Pop Land. Her job was to create magic sweets that did anything!
One sunny day, Queeny was making sweets. 'Yes!' she exclaimed, she had just made the most powerful sweet ever! Queeny placed it carefully in a glass cabinet.
That night she slept well, until she heard glass shattering. She jumped out of bed to face her arch-enemy, Kaboom! Kaboom grabbed the most magical sweet and ran out of the house. Queeny raced after him but it was too late.
'Nooo!'
Kaboom devoured the sweet!

Francesca Parker (10)
Cargilfield School, Edinburgh

Midnight Mystery

Bang! A weird creature appeared in an alleyway. It was long and had two heads, one at either end of a horse-like body that had wings sprouting out of the muscly body.

Bang! Another creature that looked like a pink, fluffy unicorn appeared as well. Then a sudden bang and a flash of dazzling yellow light. The first creature to arrive fell down dead. The unicorn lurked away.

The next morning, loads of gardens had been smashed to smithereens. Only I had an idea of who or what had done the enormous damage to all of those unfortunate gardens.

William Robert Emilius Clayton (10)

Cargilfield School, Edinburgh

Can't Get Enough

Womble was sorting out his magical pouch. His pouch held mountains of gold and diamonds. No creature could have any more riches, but Womble was greedy and mischievous. He was creeping up on the Countess of Mars, he was going to steal her purse. His fluffy, silver belly brushed the ground as he got closer to the countess. Womble pretended to be a mouse, using his mouse-like ears and tail. Womble dived into the countess' pocket, he used his platypus-like bill to grab the purse when a scent he recognised filled the air. It was his worst enemy, Three-Headed Fox...

Sophie Watts (10)
Cargilfield School, Edinburgh

Molly And Blobby

Blobby was a jelly dragon and he could also change colour. Blobby had blue eyes.
Blobby found himself in a house that he didn't recognise at all. He got so scared he turned blue! He ran into a clear door. 'Why would you make a clear door?' he asked himself.
Suddenly, the house set on fire! Blobby got really scared, he turned green! Blobby remembered that he could fly, so he said he'd better get out of the house. So Blobby flew over a forest and found a girl called Molly. Then Blobby and Molly laughed together!

Calia Miller-Salzman (10)
Cargilfield School, Edinburgh

Bramble

Once, Bramble was sitting in the shade to get away from the heat of the sun. Bramble was a big scaly creature with a lengthy tail. His eyes were sunset orange. Bramble was very well known in the town of Shroombury.
The day had come when everything was about to change. His teeth were glistening yellow.
Bramble took a stroll to his house, which was old and standing on wooden pillars. Bramble's house was scruffy. It smelt of out-of-date cheese! It was eerie and dark, the living room was mangled.
Suddenly, the door swung open with a loud bang...!

Rowan Innis Findlay (11)
Cargilfield School, Edinburgh

The Beginning Of The War For Earth

An alien called Gooey Mcdooey was travelling in space to find a new planet. Suddenly, with his super eyesight, he saw his greatest fear - Mr Mckitten! He knew what he was up to. He raced after Mr Mckitten using his speedy yellow tails. He landed on Mr Mckitten's spaceship, grabbing it with long green arms. Just as he was going to break it, an asteroid hit them, *kaboom!* Mr Mckitten fell to his doom. Gooey used his tails to land safely on planet Earth.
But out of nowhere, Mr Mckitten lunged at him with his sharp, deadly claws...

Maclean Keith (11)
Cargilfield School, Edinburgh

The Legend Of The Green Dragon

The Green Dragon is a mystical creature. It is 100 years old and it lives in a cave by a lake in Japan. The Green Dragon is guarding a sword... a sword of doom! The Sword of Doom belongs to the Black Samurai.

The sleeping dragon felt the ground begin to rumble. *The Black Samurai has returned*, he thought. He was right. The dark villain had come for the Sword of Doom.

The battle started. It was like fire and ice fighting. Finally, the amazing dragon captured the Black Samurai's spirit in the Sword of Doom for ever and ever.

Katie Henderson (10)
Cargilfield School, Edinburgh

Going To Monster School!

Spotty Fatfeet was very spotty. His feet were fat and had big, sticky pads on the bottom. His body was two red spheres and his arms were big blue ovals with six little things poking out called fingers. One day, his mum took him to school. His teacher was called Professor Slimy. At the end of the first lesson Spotty got homework. 'Nooo!' cried Spotty. Spotty tried to run away from the Planet X Primary School. He climbed out of the window, but Professor Slimy followed him. Slimy shot slime at Spotty, but missed. He got him the next time...

Finn MacGregor (9)
Cargilfield School, Edinburgh

Beyond Space

Pleh is a giant winged creature with curly horns and big eyes. But Pleh isn't in the right place. He's in a strange place called Earth.
Pleh decides one night to creep into NASA and steal one of the rockets. Pleh can breathe in space because he has been there many times. So he climbs into the rockets and blasts off! Up he flies into the dark night sky, past the stars and planets. Suddenly, there is a frightening noise. Just as Earth starts to get smaller, one of the fuel tanks bursts. How will Pleh get home?

Kinvara Nimmo (10)
Cargilfield School, Edinburgh

The Quadalopus

Once, there was the strongest creature with big abs and muscles, but he was only about the size of an ant. But he could grow to the size of a Tyrannosaurus rex.

One day, there was an earthquake. The ground shook and cracks started to form in the ground. The creature called the quadalopus was coming! He sealed up the cracks and put all the buildings back together with his super strength.

The government was so amazed that he was hired to serve in the army.

But one day, he shrank microscopic and was never seen again!

Sebastian Vardy (10)
Cargilfield School, Edinburgh

Rocket's Revenge

Rocket was heading to Butsington Village to destroy it for fun. Being a phoenix, it was easy. An hour later, it was partly destroyed. Rocket saw from his eagle eyes his arch-enemy leaping from the water to get him. He dived away just in time and the water serpent soared over his head. Rocket lashed out with his razor wings, narrowly missing him. The water serpent fired a jet of water at Rocket, hitting him in the tail. Rocket spiralled to the ground, but he got up and fired a jet of fire and magma. It hit, Rocket had won.

Callum Marryat (10)
Cargilfield School, Edinburgh

An Adventure Of A Lifetime

One day, this man walked up to me said, 'Smile,' and that changed my life. After that I was on the front of magazines, newspapers and all sorts.
I am a rather small creature with sharp pointy horns, wings, little fangs and I am able to blow fire out of my mouth. I am known as the 'crazy creature'.
But one day I began thinking, maybe there was a planet of creatures just like me? So I began building a rocket. After months of building, I had finally finished. In 3, 2, 1... blast-off!

Ellie Morrison (10)
Cargilfield School, Edinburgh

The Armless Zrote

The armless zrote loved to scare children.
One morning, it was him who got scared when he saw a griffin, it was massive! It also had eyes that stared into your soul. Perfectly dreadful. The griffin was horrible to him, he made the zrote sleep in the cold outside while he was in a warm cave.
One day, the zrote had had enough so he put a white robe over his head and lifted himself up, scaring the griffin so hard he flew away! The zrote laughed so much!
Now he enjoys scaring children and griffins!

Edward Chynoweth-Smith (10)
Cargilfield School, Edinburgh

On The Way To Take Over The Universe

Once, there was an evil fufflecorn. You wouldn't expect he was evil because he looked so, so cute! But he was on a mission to take over the universe. He was on a long walk to his secret base. His base was a cardboard box on the outskirts of town. He was nearly there when he saw around fifty runners. He had forgotten the running race! He suddenly dived to the side; if he had dived a second later, it would've been too late! Luckily he was near his box so he climbed in and pressed the button to escape.

Edward Macquaker (10)
Cargilfield School, Edinburgh

Octoslopus

Once, there lived a creature called Octoslopus. He was a purple creature with orange spots and red wings with blue dots. His eyes and legs were as green as the trees. He only had one friend called Jim. Jim had tried for two years now to get him back to his home planet, Pluto. Jim thought that this would be the day. He had invented a machine that could take you anywhere you wanted, but he only had enough fuel to go to Pluto and not back again. Jim was so scared in case Octoslopus didn't make it...

Amy Hogg (10)
Cargilfield School, Edinburgh

To Pluto

Suddenly, a spaceship came zooming out of nowhere. Benus, who was half jelly and half alien, was going to Pluto to visit friends. Suddenly, a laser came shooting past his ear. Benus looked round and saw a three-headed dog and a giant cat. They chased him back to his spaceship and Benus flew away, but he crash-landed near the three-headed dog. He got chased to a cliff, he jumped off and flew away and was never heard of again. Then the three-headed dog went back to Mars and was never heard of again either.

Jack Adams (10)
Cargilfield School, Edinburgh

Screams

Lily was a Scream. Screams are children who have big smiles and sharp teeth. Their eyes are only black, they sink right through to their sludgy brains. They can turn invisible!
One night, she crept out of the forest where she lived and slid into one of the nearby cottages. In the cottage was a boy named Jack who was sleeping quietly. Lily rolled under the bed and kept quiet. Then she got out from under the bed and grinned. She opened her mouth to scream and screamed a loud, deathly scream...!

Flora Macquaker (10)
Cargilfield School, Edinburgh

The Eating Contest

Greedon the Eater lived on the planet Eatereye.
One day, a poster went up saying: 'Eating contest,
for the best eaters on the planet'. Greedon was up
for the challenge but his arch-enemy, Fuzz-Ball the
Destroyer, also wanted to do it so Greedon had
some rivalry at the contest.
It started and they had lots of alien food and
drinks. They both made it into the final round, but
the meal was the biggest Greedon and Fuzz-Ball
had ever seen in their lives...!

Zac Dodd (10)
Cargilfield School, Edinburgh

Bobby Wobby

In a spaceship far away, there was a good, kind, nice, amazing and splendid creature called Bobby Wobby. He was very clever. He could also shape-shift and he had really big emotions. When he was sad he turned a different colour. He was also spotty. He was a fat, fluffy, loving and cuddly monster.

Edo Fox (11)
Cargilfield School, Edinburgh

Izzy And The Shoe

In a faraway land there lived a crazy creature
called Izzy. She lived in a shoe. Her friend Moshie
came over every Saturday night. They ate bunnies
and lots more.
Izzy and her friend were very sad because it was
raining. Izzy's house was an old shoe. It got so
soggy that it ripped and Izzy was worried. A wee
while later her house flooded. Izzy and Moshie
phoned the plumber then the plumber came and
Izzy realised it was her old friend Robby.
Izzy moved into a welly boot with Moshie and they
were pleased it was waterproof!

Harriet Ezady (8)
Croftmalloch Primary School, Bathgate

One Evil Day

Long ago on Saturn, there was a crazy creature called Pepo. Pepo was just about to get out of bed, but when she opened her eyes she realised her precious gold medal was gone. 'Oh no!' said Pepo. 'I think I know who stole it, it was Holly.'
Holly was a black creature with red teeth. Pepo thought Holly was horrible.
So Pepo went to find Holly, then finally she found Holly with her medal. So she fought Holly and she won.
She went home and she had hot chocolate. Pepo said, 'That is yummy!'

Alexa Macdonald (6)
Croftmalloch Primary School, Bathgate

Holly And Floss

Once, there was a crazy creature called Holly. She went to see her friend Floss, the big fat pig. She was in, they went ice skating and it was lots of fun. Then they went to McDonald's. They got a Big Mac each, they were really yummy. Then it was bedtime.

On the way back they saw their enemy, evil Peo, but she didn't see them so they jumped out at her and started to fight! Holly punched Peo in the face, then Peo ran away crying.

Holly and Floss ran back to Holly's house and watched a scary movie!

Anna Mcgilivary (7)
Croftmalloch Primary School, Bathgate

Volcano

On Tuesday, in a house on Mars, there was a crazy creature called June. She was a having a casual day until the biggest volcano in the solar system erupted.

'Arrgh!' shouted June, as lava squirted out of the volcano.

All of the other aliens ran like zebras, but June ran towards the volcano. As all the aliens ran, they looked at June and she jumped into the volcano and she saw the core of the volcano. She stopped it and saved everyone. June was a hero.

Fraser Barr (7)
Croftmalloch Primary School, Bathgate

Potato Man

Once, there was a crazy creature called Potato Man and he was eighteen. He walked around an old neighbourhood and he saw his enemy, his enemy was Burnt Potato. Potato Man punched Burnt Potato in the ear and his ear came off! 'Aargghh!' He ran home and fell asleep.

He woke up and he ate a potato, then he sat down on his chair. He went outside to Croftmall roundabout and he saw his friend Timmymabob. Potato Man did the Dab and sang his favourite song.

Mark Grant (7)
Croftmalloch Primary School, Bathgate

A Windy Day

A long time ago, on a windy Friday at 7am, BH went to the park with her friend, Water. They'd made a picnic but they forgot to take it, so they went back home. But on the way home they bumped into their enemies, Pepo, Cloudy and Holly. They had a fight and BH punched Pepo, Cloudy and Holly in their faces, BH won the fight, yay.
After the fight BH went home and sat on the couch so she could watch TV. What a day!

Miley McGivern (7)
Croftmalloch Primary School, Bathgate

The Lucky Escape

One day, a famous explorer was on a mission to explore volcanoes. He loved to explore places like waterfalls and rainforests, and many more. This time he wanted to explore a volcano. It was different for him, he'd never seen one before. Meanwhile he came to a gigantic, dangerous volcano, it was beautiful. He took lovely photographs. Then something bad happened. The volcano erupted! He panicked, he didn't know what to do.

Out of nowhere came an astonishing creature, it was amazing. It had butterfly wings, a scorpion's tail and giraffe's neck. It saved him. The explorer called it Girananeck!

Daniel Schellenberg (9)
Dollar Academy, Dollar

Waggle And The Pigeon

Slowly waking up, Waggle, the multicoloured wagglenosedig, realised that he was falling very fast. Suddenly, a fat pigeon flew up to him and started teasing him about his seven stubby legs and long blue nose!

'How could any animal look so ugly?' giggled the silly pigeon.

Poor Waggle just frowned and stared downwards. Immediately, he remembered that he was rapidly falling! Waggle glanced at the pigeon, but he was gone.

When he landed it was dark, not a single thing was to be seen. Finally, light and softness filled his body as he fell asleep in a comforting cushion factory!

Rhiannon Millar (9)
Dollar Academy, Dollar

The Flunicorn's Adventure Back Home

One day, Flunicorn was sitting watching the sky when suddenly she got transported to another world. She sat and thought about what she was going to do.

Two years later, she had made a home under a classroom table. Flunicorn was happy there until the Dark Flunicorn Force showed up. Flunicorn was not going to let them destroy her new home. So she started a small fight with the other Flunicorns. Surprisingly, they left, leaving the secret portal open. Then she climbed into it. Excitedly, Flunicorn got home and lived with her best friend, Sandy Seal. They ate marshmallows!

Madeline Spiers (9)

Dollar Academy, Dollar

A Creature Named Hairy

Once there lived a creature, not just any creature, but a hairy creature. For some strange reason he was called Hairy! Hairy thought that he was Harry Potter, so he went to Bogwarts. Hairy was rubbish at magic. Professor McFurrygle walked into Hairy's second class. Using his wand, Hairy tried to water a plant. Unfortunately, he killed the plant. Whilst trying to cast a spell, Hairy ripped a spell book. I don't think Professor McFurrygle was too impressed! Eventually, Smelldemort heard this. All he did was laugh.
But then... Hairy discovered he could fly because he had wings.

Emily Bridle (8)
Dollar Academy, Dollar

Wingsill's Adventure

Wingsill was searching for shelter, he found a desk. He went under it. His home planet of Mercury was far away.

One day he heard something drop, it was a pen. Wingsill stared, he hadn't eaten in days. Wingsill launched himself and gobbled it up. It was a teacher's marking pen.

Then another day, he sneaked up on the teacher and worked out he could turn invisible. This helped him get food.

One day he heard someone crying, he looked up and saw a child didn't have a pen. Suddenly, he became a pen! Soon he got bored. Wingsill left.

Rebecca Cowan (9)

Dollar Academy, Dollar

Creepster's Magical Adventure

Once, there was a creature called Creepster. Creepster lived in the deepest, darkest forest ever. Then one day Creepster went to find a buddy. Suddenly, he got hit by something big. Surprisingly, he was in full daylight, this was unusual. Creepster was in the human world. *Uh-oh!* he thought.
Next, Creepster remembered that he could change into any object, so he changed into a rather mysterious car and parked. Creepster changed back and walked into the forest and tried to find a buddy to play with. He finally found a friend called Billster. Billster was his buddy forever!

Fred Roemmele (9)
Dollar Academy, Dollar

The Jolly Flyers

A long time ago, Jolly Flyers lived in a land of candy and chocolate.

One day, they jumped too high and out came their very own shimmering gold wings. Sadly, there was an agreement that they would never show their special powers to humans.

Unfortunately, the next day they found there was only one Jolly Rancher left and if that happened, the Jolly Flyers would die out. As quick as a cheetah, they flew right over and got it, and doubled it up with their brilliant powers.

Every year on 31st May, they deliver Jolly Ranchers to kind children.

Rachel Newton (9)
Dollar Academy, Dollar

Billy Big Mouth

Billy was a monster with an absolutely massive mouth. He ate cars, trucks, desks, bags and schoolwork. Billy was originally from Planet Weirdo Beero, but he crashed in a school on planet Earth. Every child in the school hated Billy Big Mouth. One day, he sneaked into a classroom then the bell rang and the children went to class. Billy heard them coming. Panicked, he ate everything in the classroom and hid behind the curtain. Horrified, the children walked into the classroom. Everything was eaten! They soon realised Billy was behind the curtain, they took him out...

Charlie Kinloch (9)
Dollar Academy, Dollar

Mad Mayhem

Piggy Wiggy Woo Woo was going on a picnic when his best friend Wogeei made him laugh. He went bananas with laughter because ever since he was a baby, he always laughed this much. They were having a picnic next to the Sea of Muddy Mess! Wogeei knew what that meant... Piggy Wiggy Woo Woo jumped into the sea, still mad with laughter. 'Whee!' he shouted, but before Wogeei could look, he had disappeared into the muddy, brown water! Menacingly, a figure arose from the water! Piggy Wiggy Wo Woo had turned into a cycloplot... 'Aarrgghh!' shouted the monster...

Peter James Daniels (9)
Dollar Academy, Dollar

Zonk The Small Creature!

Zonk rolled and rolled after being attacked by a flying monster. His little arms and legs scrunched up to make a ball-like shape. Finally, he stopped and his arms and legs unfolded. He looked around. There was no sign of home. There was no noise. Zonk used his crazy creature power to find a way home.

Suddenly, the flying monster started swooping and circling him. Quickly, Zonk turned into a hard ball and started rolling faster and faster, getting smaller and smaller.

Zonk suddenly saw a cave! He quickly rolled into the entrance and then he saw Zoggyland. Hooray!

Hannah Watson (9)
Dollar Academy, Dollar

The Journey Of Spealion

Spealion was an explorer so he went on a long journey to find an uninhabited planet. Spealion is called that because he is part lion, eagle and spider.

On his way through the asteroid belt, his spaceship got hit. Spealion got knocked out and slowly headed towards Earth.

Spealion woke up and he'd crashed in the Highlands. People saw the ship but Spealion managed to get away. Spealion was in danger, so he hid but the whole world knew that he was on Earth. Spealion couldn't phone home. Thankfully, Spealion didn't get caught and made it home eventually.

Matthew Riddell-Dillet (9)

Dollar Academy, Dollar

The Magic Monkey Clown

One day, Rick was roaming downtown looking for something to buy. He stopped and looked at this gem. He picked it up, *booom!* He just turned into the Magic Monkey Clown.

The next day, he performed a show in Bling City. His first trick was going inside his immense cannon. Unfortunately, his cannon went out of control and landed in a beautiful rainforest. An evil gorilla found him. He ran up a tree, doing parkour to show off.

Suddenly, Master Clown came and said, 'Use your powers.'

So he took his diablo and killed the gorilla!

Finn Verhoeven (9)
Dollar Academy, Dollar

A Long Trip To Planet Earth

One day long, long ago, a big monster called Gobblemouth came to a peaceful little place called Schoolville. She went there to eat lots of male teachers! After she'd had a few teachers she moved to another school, then another, then another and another!
Next, she wondered if her family were missing her because they were still on planet Gobble. Gobblemouth could hypnotise people too.
But then, out of the mist, she was attacked by lots of *male teachers!*
Suddenly, her amazing, awesome, wonderful and nice family came and saved her!

Zuzu Rose Kennedy Johnston (9)
Dollar Academy, Dollar

The Snozduggler And Bob The Boy

In the darkest of nights, a little boy called Bob was woken from Dreamland...

Woah! A friendly Snozduggler appeared! Immediately, he whizzed Bob to Snoz City, which was very colourful, just like the Snozduggler. Bob laughed and enjoyed the adventure until they found a dark house which was full of Snozdugglers, but they looked scary and were being very naughty. Bob felt terrified and did not want to go in.

Bob was so frightened that he started to wake and was relieved when he realised it had just been a dream... or had it? Would the Snozduggler return?

Blair Gallagher (9)
Dollar Academy, Dollar

Word Worm

One day, a school went on a school trip to the Botanic Gardens. Suddenly, a worm crawled into the teacher's bag and then sneaked into the library with his colour-changing skin. He started going through the books and changing the words in them when the old, grumpy librarian wasn't looking. The teachers started to complain and moan.

Later that day, a boy called Joey found out so he took the book-changing worm home and copied the books. The worm had changed and became top of the class. After school, he became a world-class children's author.

Adam Kennedy (9)
Dollar Academy, Dollar

A Horrible Dream

Jack fell asleep and thought about his party, it was going to be the greatest party! There was cake and presents, but little did he know that around the corner the Dream Destroyer was hiding. Just when he was blowing out his candles, the Dream Destroyer jumped out and destroyed the cake and turned his friends into zombies! Just when Jack thought nothing could get worse, the fantastic room turned into a strange and wicked room!
At that very moment, a Fluffpuff came and sprayed magical dust everywhere. In the blink of an eye, everything was amazing again!

Cameron Fensom (9)
Dollar Academy, Dollar

The Google-Eyed Dodosaur

There was once a crazy creature, but this was not an ordinary creature, it was a monster called the Google-Eyed Dodosaur. He was about four feet tall with brown feathers, a red tail and a yellow beak and he lived in the coastal or swamp areas in Africa.

One amazing day, he went travelling. Immediately, a local tribe heard about the monster. A search party set out to find the monster, suddenly they saw something extraordinary and they rushed over and there he was!

This story has been told for generations and people still believe it to this day.

Grace McCaig (9)
Dollar Academy, Dollar

The Greatest Fight In All Of China

One day, a creature lived in the ocean of China. People had been attacked and never come back. The ocean was dark and mysterious. The people started seeing the creature, they described it as orange, green and blue, with a fire symbol. They called him Godzilla.

They had another sighting and there was an egg, but it was not Godzilla's egg. It hatched and started destroying China. The army tried to kill it, but another one came, it was the mother. After she came, Godzilla attacked with fire power. He camouflaged himself then shape-shifted as well.

Aadam Hussain (9)
Dollar Academy, Dollar

The Zigolars

One day, I started losing items. This happened to everyone. Fortunately, I saw something. I described it to my amazing teacher. It had two heads, six legs, eight ears and was blue, orange, pink, yellow, red and green. I named it a Zigolar! Suddenly, it dashed across the room to my friend. The Zigolar bit him and he turned into a Zigolar! By the end of the day everyone was Zigolars! I was the only human left!

As quiet as a mouse, I went to an alley, but there were over one hundred Zigolars.

'No! I'm a Zigolar!' I shrieked.

Ian Menzies (9)

Dollar Academy, Dollar

SlimySim's Journey To A Human House

Once, there was a crazy creature called SlimySim. SlimySim lived in Slime Land, but he was making a journey to a human house. He finally made it. 'Now for the hard part,' he said. He wanted to go to a human house because he wanted to scare people. First, he jumped into a jelly bowl and as soon as human came, they screamed and ran away. 'Great!' said SlimySim. 'I am nailing this!' After a little bit, a dog came. Dogs are SlimySim's enemies so he went, 'Grrr, get away!' and chased the poor dog away!

April Methven (9)
Dollar Academy, Dollar

One Boy's Bidding

'Do my bidding and you shall be rewarded,' hissed a black puff of smoke, taking the form of a young boy.

Scared, one of the two men beside him refused. There was a flash of light and he lay on the floor, dead. Apprehensively, the other man, James, left the room in search of a boy. He travelled only by night in the blustering shadows of the darkness, until one day he found the boy. He summoned the creature. Everything went cold, like the happiness had gone from the world. It touched the boy, screamed and disappeared into thin air.

India Stevens (9)
Dollar Academy, Dollar

Chip And The Deli

Slowly Chip woke up, opened her curtains and realised that it was the day she was going shopping with her best friend, Grape. Grape could fall apart and put herself back together again. She was like a jigsaw. When they reached the shops they shopped madly and finished as quick as you could click your fingers. But there was one shop they hadn't been to - the deadly Tesco! As slick and quick as they could they spotted their worst enemy, Spice, so they grabbed what they wanted and bolted. Grabbing crisps, Chip loved hers so much she blew up!

Emma Jane Wallace (9)
Dollar Academy, Dollar

Life On Earth

One day, a sponge creature was on Jupiter. He wondered if he could go to Earth. He decided to sneak into his dad's rocket. He didn't know how to fly, he tried to find the big start button but just couldn't find it! Finally, he found it and that second he went flying up into the sky! Then he switched it off and on again, trying to get directly to Earth. It was confusing!

He finally got there and straight away he heard beautiful birds singing. He sucked all the water into the ground.

'Oh no!' said a little boy.

Zac Taylor (9)
Dollar Academy, Dollar

The Mini Elephantant!

One bright day in the deep, dark rainforest, there was a girl called Ava who was searching for the rarest insect in the world. Suddenly, she stopped to listen for the elephantant! She saw it right at her left toe, then the mini elephantant crawled up her sleeve and whispered into her ear. Then the ant crawled back to the den he'd made just for Ava. As she walked to the den, the door got bigger so she could go inside and see the amazing, extraordinary ant life. She was speechless and mind-blown by all the amazing elephantants!

Ava Taylor (9)
Dollar Academy, Dollar

The Two Happy Pigs

The three-tailed Chinese mini pig flew mountain to mountain, visiting all his friends. Every time he flew he made a rainbow behind him. At the end of each rainbow there was a pot of gold. He flew all over the world, especially to Scotland and Africa.
One day, he flew all the way to Japan and his enemy, the three-tailed Japanese flying mini pig, found the gold. The three-tailed Chinese flying mini pig was not annoyed. He was glad that someone had found his pot of gold and they both became friends. They lived happily ever after!

George Livingstone Irvine (9)
Dollar Academy, Dollar

Miggle Moo

Miggle Moo suddenly crash-landed in Dollar Playground. Everyone heard a bang, I was the only one who could see Miggle Moo. Then he jumped out of his spaceship and I was staring at this big, fat, ugly monster who was now walking over to the school. Suddenly, he jumped onto the roof and through the window to the cloakroom. He ate all the homework in the school bags! Miggle Moo liked homework!

Ten minutes later, he'd eaten all the homework he could find. He then went and got his spaceship repaired, then flew home to Moo Moo Land.

Monty Smith (9)
Dollar Academy, Dollar

Welcome To Earth

Five Eyes walked along with his two dragon-like feet, slimy body, sharp claws, pointy teeth, dark blue wings and five eyes. Five Eyes walked to his spaceship to fly to Earth to find lots of food because he hadn't had breakfast. So he went to Earth. He landed his spaceship carefully. He tried not to get caught by humans. He sneaked into Dollar Academy, but Mrs Murphy caught Five Eyes, he was scared! She didn't know what he was so she phoned the police, but Five Eyes ran away. Mrs Murphy chased Five Eyes to his spaceship...

Aaryn Mckenna (9)
Dollar Academy, Dollar

Gargorg's Bad Day

Gargorg was a greedy creature who lived on Cloud Nine Hundred and Five. He loved to steal shiny treasure. He did this with his SHTM (Super Hoover Tornado Maker) which was a Hoover that made tornadoes. Gargorg was a green creature with four eyes and wings. There was only one thing he hated - policemen!

One day, he was using his SHTM over London. Whilst watching the Creatures of the Day, he accidently sucked up a policeman! The policeman saw the treasure and decided to arrest Gargorg. That is why you should never steal!

Hamish Ferguson (9)
Dollar Academy, Dollar

Oddy The Octopus

Once upon a time there was an octopus, his name was Oddy. He lived a lonely life in Lake Lubbadub, because of his looks with his blue tentacles and yellow spots.

This was until one night when the night monsters came. He tried to warn everybody but they didn't wake up until he realised he was glowing like a red beacon and had already saved everybody. So then all the fish crowned him King Oddy, but not just King Oddy, King Oddy the Eveready.

From that day on he promised to keep all the fish safe and watch over them.

Elena Beverland (9)
Dollar Academy, Dollar

The Germ Worm's Bad Day!

The dark green germ worm had sharp teeth and massive hands and feet (for giving people flu and colds). That was what he did every day.

He was sneaking up on a little girl to give her the flu, when suddenly... his elephant-like hands and feet fell off! The germ worm was devastated and he started crying out of his six eyes!

'If only I had never started making people sick, if only I hadn't been so mean to soap and water. If only I had never grown out my hands and feet, they would never have fallen off!'

Victoria Cara Murphy (9)
Dollar Academy, Dollar

The Adventures Of Grapedo

A long time ago, a grape went to the Antarctic. Grape got amazingly big and fat as it was so cold! He decided to go to a hotter place, the Sahara Desert! He stayed there for three years until something started to happen again... He got very wrinkly and started to shrivel up! He got smaller, which meant only one good thing: he was now super speedy and whenever he took a shower he became a grape again.

He had the best life ever, he loved it so much. Which is why everybody in the world called him Super Grapedo!

Oscar Parkins (8)
Dollar Academy, Dollar

The Big Journey

The Kabrospike was lost and didn't know where to go. He was in the middle of nowhere. Kabrospikes do not like butterflies or anything happy and joyful. He had to get back home whilst avoiding those things. So he set off. He had a map so he hoped he could find the way.
He suddenly got surrounded by butterflies, it was like a rainbow had exploded! There was too much colour! Kabrospike fainted on top of the butterflies. When he woke up he was back on Neptune. He was finally home with his family.

Xavier Ndoumbe (9)
Dollar Academy, Dollar

Joey's Day

Once upon a time there was a land called Planet Cheesy Tomatoes and there was a famous creature called Joey. He could eat one hundred million tomatoes in five seconds! He had some enemies who were cheesy vegetables. They were bad things.

One day, Joey was eating a burger for a change, when the evil vegetables attacked him... So Joey ran and the vegetables chucked tomatoes, but they were cheesy so they did not hurt him at all. He got his cheesy launchers out and fired and all the cheesy vegetables ran away.

Bobby Shearer (9)
Dollar Academy, Dollar

The Mindmaster's Escape

The Mindmaster was sitting in his classroom getting more intelligence into his huge brain. The Mindmaster was a tiny person, he was probably the size of a pea! Soon the Mindmaster got to a hard question, which was very easy for him! He could sense a spider nearby. The Mindmaster was really scared because the Mindmaster was incredibly small! The Mindmaster ran to hide on the teacher's desk. He watched the spider go back to its web in shame! The Mindmaster went back to his maths at the big, cosy table.

Callum Robinson (9)
Dollar Academy, Dollar

Goggle-Eyed Gooshooter And The Big Pot Of Goo

Once, there was a creature called Goggle-Eyed Gooshooter. He lived in Gooland. He had four eyes, six legs and holes in his body to shoot goo out of! One day, his goo ran out so he went to get more but there was none left! After that he went to the next shop along. It had a gigantic pot of goo. He wondered how to get it. After a few moments, he remembered he could slide under the door. Next, he slid under the huge door, he got past the lasers and got the gigantic pot of sticky, green goo.

Rosie Grace Everington (9)
Dollar Academy, Dollar

Gary The Gargoyle

Gary was panting, he was running so fast he was a blur. He couldn't see the humans behind him. But there was a problem, he had run out of his invisibility juice. The air passed his sleek fur. Gary was one of a kind. He was a one-eyed gargoyle. He turned a corner, there was a dead end. The more he ran the more he wanted to turn around and go home. Gary turned and saw the humans had snuck up behind him and fired nets from guns. Gary was stuck. The gargoyle tried to spread his wings. Gary died.

Adam Howat (9)
Dollar Academy, Dollar

Spots

Spots was born on Pluto. Every single coloured spot on him was related to a poison.

He came to Earth from Pluto to find something to eat and drink. All the humans thought Spots was very ugly, horrible and hairy, so Spots decided to turn invisible. Next, he went to get food and drink. They couldn't see Spots because of his invisibility. He stole all the food and drink. Then he pretended to work and stole all the money, and took it back to his homeland after trying to battle humans.

Fin Patchett (9)
Dollar Academy, Dollar

Plunger's Escape

Plunger could be found in your tap. But one day he saw a man coming. Plunger was squishy, bumpy and could disguise himself, so the man could not see him. He was carrying a new tap! Plunger stopped and thought. Plunger had never been out of this tap before.

The man turned it on then Plunger swished out of the tap; all Plunger could hear was spunglings sucking up water. Plunger was made out of water so the spunglings jumped to get him. Luckily, Plunger got to the toilet seat!

Marley Haston (9)
Dollar Academy, Dollar

Mr Fluffball

Mr Fluffball was a massive walking fluffball with a club, a massive mouth, nine eyes and dragon feet and a tail. He was very nice. But the problem was that everyone thought that he would eat them! Also, he could break anything.

One day, he met a kind, wise man and he and Mr Fluffball became friends. Then the townspeople saw the wise man with Mr Fluffball and the whole town became friends with Mr Fluffball, who was now the most popular person in the town!

Louis Di Mascio (9)
Dollar Academy, Dollar

Gold's Crazy Adventures

Gold is half angel and half devil, she can fly with her magnificent, soft angel wings and can cast spells and go invisible!
Slugs are all over Cloudypufflandia and Gold's best friend is a cool slimy slug, his name is King Barry. But there is a war going on, they have to battle! Slashdeebashes are attacking Cloudypufflandia, but Gold and King Barry's slug army are stronger than the Slashdeebashes' army. All of the baby slugs have to be evacuated!
Soon the war is over and they celebrate winning by throwing a magical party, and they also eat delicious rainbow cake!

Grace Simm (10)
Echline Primary School, South Queensferry

The Horns

Urgently, Heatwave chases Furture with his eight weak legs. He reaches for the gold magical horns with his blue wings. He misses, then he has a magnificent idea. Heatwave throws a stink bomb then Furture stops and starts to cough, then Heatwave steals the horns but Furture starts to use his power, but then Heatwave makes a deal. The deal is if Furture gives Heatwave the horns then Heatwave will be Furture's slave. Furture accepts.

'Fan me,' orders Furture. So Heatwave does then Heatwave uses his horns and magics away.

'I'm coming for you,' shouts Furture!

Issy Wood (9)
Echline Primary School, South Queensferry

Flimba's Mission

Scattered pieces of cat and robot body parts lay around the isolated lab of Dr Gilony as he finished his masterpiece: a robot with cat DNA or, in other words, Flimba.

Finally, Dr Gilony stepped away from his desk to reveal an ugly, deformed creature. It was almost like a cat, but not. Then mechanically she sat up without any expression.

Reluctantly, Dr Gilony started to smile then chuckle, then he gave out an ear-splitting cackle. He gave Flimba her first order... to destroy the world. She got up and shape-shifted into an elephant and started to crush the Earth...

Ella Kirsty Balanowski (10)
Echline Primary School, South Queensferry

Spy Spirit

Spirit is a critter from Buglandia, her people and king had sent her to secretly spy on an absolutely tiny land called Culumbug. It was a long way to go but Spirit made it to Randy's (the king's) castle. Surprisingly the castle was bigger than the land. Finally, Spirit found the information she needed so she fluttered home to Buglandia.

When she got back, the many people from her town greeted Spirit with joy. Spirit got awarded a beautiful award for doing a fantastic job. Spirit got to stay in an extremely posh hotel and had cake every single day!

Eva Blair (10)
Echline Primary School, South Queensferry

Rappin' Robots

Rapsterbot walked down the valley of the shadow of death, spreading his beats from side to side. 'His palms were sweaty, knees weak, arms were heavy...' rapped Rapsterbot.
'Your rapping is weak!'
'Oh look who it is. Gangsterbot!' said Rapsterbot. 'I was going to challenge you to a rap battle, but okay...'
Rapsterbot roared so loud that it knocked him down and whilst he had a chance, he jumped on his Harley Davidson and zoomed off with a top speed of 105 miles per hour. Rapsterbot zoomed off into the dark, gloomy distance.

Elliot Murphy (10)
Echline Primary School, South Queensferry

Crazy Creature!

Startled, Splanky awoke from a dreaded nightmare. He hauled himself out of bed. He had dreamt that he started his new job as a dreamcatcher and he made a young child's dream a nightmare.

As he caught the bus he met a gentle Cyclops named Jerald, he was also a dreamcatcher. Quickly, they got off the bus and Jerald gave Splanky the secret code to the headquarters of dream making. That's when he met Smoosh who became his work partner.

Later on that night, Smoosh and Jerald flew back to Splanky's house and had cake and juice. They lived happily.

Emily Simm (10)
Echline Primary School, South Queensferry

Potato Man V Donald Trump

Potato Man had been put in a vicious battle with Jeffrey, his enemy for life. The fight lasted all night until Donald Trump interrupted. He kneed Potato Man in the face! Potato Man went hospital and was told Donald Trump had gone to prison, but Potato Man wanted to fight Donald Trump!
Their fight was legendary. Potato Man breathed fire at Donald Trump, then Donald Trump used his long arms to his advantage. Donald Trump was weak, Potato Man started to destroy Donald Trump, Trump was getting nervous. Potato Man taunted Donald Trump.
Who would be victorious?

James Yule (10)
Echline Primary School, South Queensferry

The Assassination

Six Arms strolled away from his UFO then used his supersonic jump to jump all the way to Moustache Kingdom. When he arrived he needed to knock out two guards, then he used his blasters to explode the door open. Afterwards, he needed to use his purple scales to blend into things. Six Arms went into the centre of the kingdom, which was colossal. 'Right, I need to find that evil Moustache King,' muttered Six Arms.

There he was, right in the centre with golden, shiny, sparkly armour on.

'Say goodnight, Moustache King!' said Six Arms...

Luke Collins (10)

Echline Primary School, South Queensferry

Platof's Blast-Off!

Platof is a Hudangus. A Hudangus has purple skin with green swirls. They also have blue, square, floppy ears that help them float. They have green, deformed arms, a diamond-shaped pink chest and triangle legs. Platof was born on Neptune on 30th December 2321.

Platof plodded to the Earth launcher with his brother, sister, mum and dad. Platof got to go inside the gigantic rocket because his dad, Smerlocke, worked there! Platof was so excited that he whacked the big red button that said 'launch'!

'10, 9... 4, 3, 2, 1... lift-off!'

James Mills (10)

Echline Primary School, South Queensferry

My Crazy Creature Destiny

One day Destiny, the cute, little, fluffy, googly-eyed monster, went to the ice cream shop to get her favourite dessert. As soon as she got there she bumped into a friendly monster. He had sticky pads on his feet. He was really hairy and a bit stinky, but that didn't matter. He had a cute little antenna too.

Destiny loved making new friends, so she bounced up to him. She was really kind to the monster and offered him some ice cream. The monster said, 'No thanks.' Destiny didn't mind though, she asked if he wanted to visit her home.

Tegan MacPherson (10)
Echline Primary School, South Queensferry

Smosh's Story

'No! I want to watch the football!' said Smosh.
'Well, I want to watch the X Factor!' said Splash.
Smosh trudged to his room to pack. He had two
short wings, four spiky fangs and a cat's tongue.
The next day he was gone!
Smosh strode hundreds of miles, high and low, his
stinky feet got dragged all over the place.
Suddenly, something stopped him and told him he
had to fight. He got giant spotty feet in his face
and sharp claws in his stomach, however he won.
Smosh ran home and made up with Splash.

Freya Ridgway (10)
Echline Primary School, South Queensferry

Camb's Crazy Story

Camb had woken up to find himself on the sofa, ready for his first day at space school. When he arrived there he found that he was different and when he finally got into class, trudging on his lumpy foot and his sort of normal foot, he realised that everyone treated him differently too. He eventually came up with the idea of becoming invisible, but when he tried someone saw him and started playing with him, and from then on Camb didn't feel different, even though different was good. He never listened to negative thoughts again, ever.

Zak Mclaren (10)
Echline Primary School, South Queensferry

The Assassination

Reluctantly, Jeffery walked into the small escape pod. It shot off and after what seemed like months he landed on a very green planet. Some people came and took him away to a weird location. It said 51 everywhere and there were a lot of screens all over the place. They strapped Jeffery to a seat and put a light in his face. The first thing they said to him was, 'Where are you from? Have you got any superpowers?'

'Yes, why?' he replied.

'We need you to kill Donald Trump.'

So he went to America...

Aran Hay (10)
Echline Primary School, South Queensferry

Boss-A-Tron's Story

Boss-A-Tron got made at a factory called The Monster Maker. He had blue dragon wings with a robot body and a giant snakeskin tail. Last but not least, he had two alien eyes sticking out of his head and a black and bright green top hat. He lived on Planet Oooh and 'Oooh' was his favourite word. He had a spaceship.

One day it was about to get bombed, but he used his lasers to destroy the other ship, then he saw his enemy Mr Chan in the sky with a parachute. Bye-bye!

Boss-A-Tron lived a happy life.

Robbie Ferguson (10)
Echline Primary School, South Queensferry

My Crazy Creature Land

One day, there was a little crazy creature, an alien, it went into a forest. The alien used her ten googly eyes to see what was in the green forest. Also she used her invisible nose as she was flying high in the blue wintery, snowy sky.

All of a sudden there was a big noise, the alien didn't want to look back after. A fierce monster was heading towards her, she didn't know what to do. So she landed and hid in a bunch of bushes until the crazy monster was gone far, far away from the beautiful forest.

Eve Falconer (10)
Echline Primary School, South Queensferry

The King Pikachu Wins

King Pikachu couldn't go and take out the Charmander army because he was feeling too ill to go out and fight, so five Pikachu recruits went to take them out.

Eventually it was time to fight, fearfully the team got their powers fully charged! Three, two, one, charge!

Bang! Bang! Bang! their powers went.

Meanwhile, when they were fighting, a pack of the Pikachu team flanked the Charmanders. The armies went down so fast there was only two recruits left, and finally the Pikachu army won.

Owen Morrison (10)

Echline Primary School, South Queensferry

The Crazy Creature

Suddenly, Coco Bolla woke up but hold on... she woke up on planet Earth! The red-striped, rainbow-winged, colour-changing spotted body and two-nosed creature couldn't believe where she was. She looked around but nothing, absolutely nothing was made out of sweets, like on her planet.
As soon as Coco Bolla's three huge eyes turned around, a very pretty girl grabber her attention. Coco opened her four hands to greet the girl. Then, without warning, they appeared on Coco Bolla's planet...

Zuzia Karusewicz (10)
Echline Primary School, South Queensferry

Rainbow Fajita's Adventure

'Where am I? How did I get here? Wait, I'm in the North Pole!' Rainbow Fajita glanced with her powerful eyes at the amazing Santa's grotto. She skipped and met Santa, although Santa didn't act like himself.

'Oh no, it's King Allan Hitler, my biggest enemy!' She fought him amazingly with her spotty, multicoloured hands. All of the elves were part of the king's gang.

'Stop! Stop! *Stoopp!*' yelled Rainbow Fajita, as she fell to the ground...

Ciara Morris (9)
Echline Primary School, South Queensferry

The Enemy On Mars

Fuzzle went to Mars and made three friends, one with blue fur, one with purple fur and one with pink fur. The one with pink fur was called Splodge, the one with blue fur was called Spidge and the purple one was Fluffpuff.

But Splodge attacked Fuzzle and punched Fuzzle in the eye, so Fuzzle was super angry and shot Splodge with his laser eye beams. Splodge cried. The next day, Fuzzle said sorry and Splodge said sorry too. They recovered from the incident, then Fuzzle headed home.

Niamh Jack (9)
Echline Primary School, South Queensferry

Nancy In Trouble!

Nancy was a huge pink monster with the greenest plants you'll ever see poking out of her head. She was a naughty girl and never had the time for anyone or anything, she even forgot about her puppy Lexi, so her mum had to look after it, her mum walked the dog 24/7 and bathed it. Her mum wanted to get her back by pranking her. She got a fake cat and dog and laid them in a basket. Nancy heard a knock on the door. She picked up the basket and cared for the fake animals!

Ava Laing (9)
Echline Primary School, South Queensferry

Naughty Timmy!

Timmy was a cute but scary baby monster! He was so naughty when it was bath time and also dinner time. He put mud on his dinner and mud in his bath under his bubbles. Every time he was bad he grew another eye and his mum thought he was ill! So she took him to the doctor but he said he didn't have an illness, so she took him home for a nap. The next day, he went to the park and he made a friend and they played for hours. Timmy changed and was good forever.

Cerys Brett (9)
Echline Primary School, South Queensferry

Weird People!

Splodge, the fluffy yeti, ran away as her parents had told her off. She ran far, far away, but she got scared. She walked up to a mermaid called Ariel who had five eyes and asked, 'How far is it to Rainbow Pole?' Ariel said it was a mile away. Splodge was scared, the people there were so different. So she plodded to the shop and bought an umbrella and made her way back to her home and apologised, and then gave her mum and dad a big hug and went to bed.

Helen Latta (9)
Echline Primary School, South Queensferry

Crazy Creature

Ronny dragged his big, fuzzy arms along the wet ground and went to Hillary Cricket (his boss). He had to slaughter Donald Dump, so he set out and bought a bazooka. His snake-like skin made him impossible to see. He held the bazooka over his shoulder and *bang!* Donald Dump was gone! Hillary was going to be president, but it turned out that Ronny had shot the wrong guy! The police were behind him. Ronny was sentenced to life!

Michael Glanville (9)
Echline Primary School, South Queensferry

Cookie Crunch And The Terrible Teacher

Cookie Crunch jumped in a backpack and then something lifted the backpack and when it had stopped moving, Cookie Crunch jumped out. Cookie Crunch ended up in a classroom, Cookie Crunch was starving. Right beside Cookie Crunch was a delicious smell, it was another cookie! So Cookie Crunch ate it. Suddenly, the door opened and it was a teacher, so Cookie Crunch acted dead. The teacher picked Cookie Crunch up and started to eat him! But luckily the teacher only ate a bit of him so Cookie Crunch was still alive. Cookie Crunch got back in the backpack happily!

Mirryn Fergusson (9)
Georgetown School, Dumfries

Paccy's Got A Problem

One day, Paccy noticed he was locked out of his arcade. He was worried so he looked for a way in, but everything was locked so he slept outside all night.

The next day was Sunday, but the arcade was closed on Sundays. He found something to open a window, but unfortunately it just snapped. He felt really miserable.

The next morning when the arcade opened, he went to open the door but he wasn't heavy enough. He saw an open window. He was excited. He piled up boxes to jump on and finally made it back into his home.

Ryan William Rodgers (9)
Georgetown School, Dumfries

Unicorn Madness

About 2.5 million years ago, a unicorn was sitting on her beautiful rainbow rug when she heard a loud bang! She vanished and when she reappeared she suspiciously looked around the strange land. The unicorn gasped! A few moments passed and she lasered down eighteen trees. She felt bad. After that she saw one of her old friends, it was Candy Apple! Was she imagining it? The unicorn remembered Candy Apple wanted revenge, so she ran and ran, but there was a lady who picked her up and tried to eat her so unicorn lasered her...

Amy Johnston (9)
Georgetown School, Dumfries

Halo And The Fairies

It all started when Halo was looking for some friends, so she went to an arcade. Halo was jealous of all the creatures in the games, so she went through one of the thin cables and talked to them because the arcade was closed. She talked to those in the 'Weather', game but they had too many friends already. So she asked Flamey, but he said no because he would burn her. So she asked the fairies, they said yes, on one condition... the fairies wanted to stay with Halo in her tree. Halo said yes. They became best friends!

Clara Elizabeth Conchar (9)
Georgetown School, Dumfries

The Phone Thief

Yesterday, I met a hand-shaped monster with gloopy stuff on him.
Last night he came mischievously into my room and made a disgraceful mess! When I came to get dressed, I saw a massive mess then I went down the stairs and back up and it was clean!
I went downstairs to watch TV and I saw the hand glooper freak again and it had my bed covers. It went into the dining room then I heard rustling from under the table. The hand glooper freak was playing with my special phone that was shiny and sparkly!

Joe Alison (8)
Georgetown School, Dumfries

Footy World

One day there was a monster called Footy, he was a vicious monster. When football players were playing a match, he stole all the balls to make a colossal football stew. Once, a Liverpool player saw him and he came to the surface and scared everyone off the pitch. The referee was not scared so Footy ate him for lunch! He ran after the football players because they were his worst enemies in the whole wide world.

Footy started to think that chasing people was wrong, so he decided to change...

Aiden Stewart Mcculloch (9)
Georgetown School, Dumfries

Bad Monster

In 2004, there was a monster. Dabster landed on Earth, and Dabster played a game of football. After the game Dabster broke the law and so was sent to jail. Then Dabster escaped from jail and he started exploding cars and houses, but then he got shot. But Dabster went invisible so he didn't get hit.
After that, Dabster turned into a giant then Dabster ate four hundred people!
He went into a hotel and fell and broke his leg, and after that he was sent back to his home planet.

Evan Robertson (9)
Georgetown School, Dumfries

Scared Of The Dentist

There was a boy called Ben who had a monster under his bed called Doda who had very dirty teeth because he didn't like the dentist. Ben always asked why, but Doda never answered.
One day, Ben told Doda if he went he would get him an ice cream. Doda said okay. Ben had a very hard job getting him in the car, but eventually he went in. Ben waited for a long time.
When Doda came back out he had a toothbrush. Ben was really proud of him so he gave him some yummy chocolate ice cream.

Katie Aitchison (8)
Georgetown School, Dumfries

Monster Friend

One day, there was a little monster who was very hairy and he took a walk a lot of the time.
On 5th December, he was taking a walk when he saw a big monster and they played together. Then they had his favourite food, eggs and eyes!
On Friday, he went to the giant monster's house, but he wasn't there so he went to the shop and found him. The giant monster was fighting with another monster so he helped his friend. Then the other monster wanted to be friends with them too.

Jack Trosh (9)
Georgetown School, Dumfries

I Found A Crazy Creature - Mr Fire Freak

One day after school, I met a crazy creature. He was Mr Fire Freak. I let him stay in my shed. I told my mum there was a crazy creature called Mr Fire Freak, but he wasn't really a freak he was actually really nice. My mum stood still before she fell to the ground and passed out!

Then Mr Fire Freak wanted to do something so we went to the mall for some shopping. Mr Fire Freak was amazed by the mall. Then Mr Fire Freak saw the police and the police put Mr Fire Freak in jail!

Junior Pinnock (9)
Georgetown School, Dumfries

People Scare The Big Monster

Jermy Jim lived inside a pole. One day, he was walking and a person saw him and called the police, so he ran but then he got caught. Finally, he got away and he was happy. He started breaking stuff, then he saw a person and got scared and ran away. After that, he saw more people and he jumped on a massive building and started going crazy. He jumped into a big pool and started swimming away, then he got out of the pool and he was okay.
He moved on to the next town...

Fahad Gazi (9)
Georgetown School, Dumfries

The Ocean Bug Pet

I was on my boat and a monster jumped on. We sailed to shore and he turned into a bug and followed me home. Suddenly, he turned back into himself. I asked him his name and he said he was Dashing Dave. I tried to take him back, but whenever he went to the ocean he would always follow me home again.

The next time he followed me home he didn't turn into a bug, instead he squirted me with some slime. As soon as he squirted me I decided to keep him forever!

Caethon Mutch (9)

Georgetown School, Dumfries

The Mini Story Of Lucky Unicorn Star

One day, under the rainbow, there was a crazy creature called Lucky Unicorn Star. She was just playing around when an evil monster did a magic spell on Lucky Unicorn Star! The spell made her right hand go big, but the spell went a bit wrong (luckily in a good way because it also made her right hand lucky!). She could wave her right hand and she would give good luck to whoever she was waving it at. But it didn't always go to plan...

Morven Kirk (8)
Georgetown School, Dumfries

Five-Eyed Bill

Five-Eyed Bill was a crazy, crazy creature. He had the ability to make things dark for humans.
Once, he came and sneaked into a school. He was in a massive classroom and in his head he said, 'Brilliant! I can scare them all!'
Later, he saw a human and the monster started a fight and Five-Eyed Bill was able to turn everything dark and scare the human and win the fight.

Billy Gray (8)
Georgetown School, Dumfries

Twin Monsters

One sunny day on the planet Sparkle, Big Twinny went invisible. Little Twinny couldn't find Big Twinny. Little Twinny went all over the planet looking for him, then she went invisible too. They both came back, wondering why they had changed. Then they shouted, 'What happened? I'm all fluffy!'

The next day, both Twinnies went to a castle where people laughed at them!

They said, 'We don't care, you're stinky!' and they left. They decided to cheer themselves up and they got a chippy, it was delicious. By bedtime they had full tummies and fell asleep dreaming of good friends.

Leigh Kirkpatrick (8)
Lincluden School, Dumfries

Ozzy And The Velcromen

Once, there was a purple monster called Ozzy. He had a fluffy head and body, blue arms and polka-dot legs. He absolutely hated velcro and vegetables! He lived in a hut with his little brothers Oscar, Omen and Oliver.

One day, he woke up and his brothers weren't there. He panicked. Out in the garden he noticed grey stuff on the ground. 'Oh no! It's velcro and where there's velcro there's velcromen!' That meant his brothers had been kidnapped. Magically, a unicorn appeared with his little brothers on its back. They celebrated by riding over a rainbow into the sunset.

Ethan Mcnaught (9)
Lincluden School, Dumfries

Planet Earth

Once upon a time a little creature was born. His father called him Illuminator.

After he was exposed to cosmic rays, Illuminator was abandoned by his family, then he landed on a mysterious planet called Earth. Soon he made a new friend called Betty, she was very pretty, she had eight eyes! They played together for a while. After playing, he met someone else who frightened him and made him shiver. The man punched his face, he lost some teeth. Illuminator used his laser eyes and zapped him, and he fell into a gorge and was never seen again.

Kieran Carruthers (8)
Lincluden School, Dumfries

I Want Santa!

Once upon a time there was a monster called Weerdy, he was really poor. One day, he went shopping then saw a wee boy and took him away with him. The boy's mum came back and screamed. She phoned the police and said, 'My boy's been taken!'
The police went after Weerdy, but they never caught him because he went to New York. The boy loved it but he wanted to see Santa, but the monster said no! The boy started to cry and the monster said, 'Okay we'll go and see him.'
The boy was so happy.

Cassie Mcgregor (9)
Lincluden School, Dumfries

Potato Man

I'm Potato Man and I live on Pluto.

One day, I was getting shopping and an announcement said, 'Take shelter immediately!' All the other creatures were running their hearts out. The next thing, a spaceship took them all away, now Pluto was ghost town! I was the only one there.

I decided to do some science, I love science. I made a robot that was a big marshmallow and I called him Baymax 1.0. Unfortunately it wasn't working the first time, but I fixed it and used it to bring all the creatures back.

Eilidh White (9)
Lincluden School, Dumfries

The Problem With Love

Once upon a time there was a monster called Dan who loved playing video games. I must admit, he was actually the best gamer on planet Pluto.
One night, Dan woke up from a bad dream and saw five ghosts. Dan was scared, he ran away to the bathroom to hide. Then he ran out of the house and into a girl called Cream-Puff, and he fell in love. He slowly walked past trying to look at her face, then she said, 'Hi.' Dan hoped to kiss Cream-Puff but there was one problem... his lips were stitched closed!

Kendra Bobbi Douglas (9)

Lincluden School, Dumfries

King Splat

On a nice sunny day on Paradise Island, King Splat and his son Ralph woke up and went to the Salty Store and got a tea. They decided to go swimming for five and a half hours, they got ready and soon the clock hit six o'clock and tonnes of speakers, disco lights, drinks bottles and food appeared as if by magic. So everybody had a party till 1am. Then they both fell into bed and went to sleep.
King Splat woke up and Ralph was missing, but he found him under his bed!

Mikey Warner (9)
Lincluden School, Dumfries

Kweky Saves The Day

Hi, my name is Kweky and I like doing handstands.
I can lift heavy things like houses and even my
school.
I was at school doing maths, then at playtime I
jumped over the fence and suddenly I saw a
speeding car racing towards a girl crossing the
road. Quickly, I jumped out and saved her!
Everyone was so happy with me and I was given an
award in assembly.

Kaidy Tanbini (8)
Lincluden School, Dumfries

Batty Batter Gets Scared

Batty walked along the mushy grass, his feet sweltering in the heat. He was wondering as he was going home why his feet were turning yellow; they were boiling in the weather.

All of a sudden, a big black shadow appeared over Batty. Batty was terrified and started running home, but the shadow got closer to him and jumped in front of him. It was a big black bird and it wanted to eat Batty for his dinner!

Oh no, thought Batty, *I should run for the hills fast!* Finally, the crow flew away and Batty went home safely.

Lauren Fleming (11)
Lochside School, Dumfries

The Shadowy Homework Thief

One stormy night, a boy named Josh was sound asleep. As he slept, Herobrin, a creeper-like creature, stole his homework that was on his desk. The next morning, Josh woke up and said, 'Did Mum move my homework?'

As he went into the living room, he saw his homework on the couch. To him this was strange because his mum never moved his homework!

Clank! Clank! Clank!

'What was that? It came from the basement.'

As Josh ran to the basement door he heard it again, so he leaned his ear against the old wooden door, listening...

Tyler Wilson (11)
Lochside School, Dumfries

Scaly Pretty Zoo

Although his name was Pretty, he wasn't so pretty to look at. He had scaly skin and eyes that popped! He could squeeze through the smallest of spaces and could fly anywhere he wanted.

Pretty squeezed into the smallest hole in the gate to enter the zoo. It was so peaceful, but he didn't like the quiet so he decided to cause some mayhem!

The first thing Pretty saw was the lions' den, he unlocked the gate and cast a spell to make the lions invisible. The lions chased scaly, scared, sorry Pretty out of the dark zoo!

Destinee Xiomara Houston (11)

Lochside School, Dumfries

Jupi

Jupi was adorable and soft and also very mysterious. When a human came close he would run off to a hiding spot and wait until they were gone.
One day, someone spotted Jupi and started following him to the mansion down the street. A girl found Jupi and picked him up and tickled his soft, furry foot, then put him down. Jupi gave a soft smile and ran away.
But outside a wild animal catcher caught Jupi and put him in a cage, then took him away. But before he put Jupi in his van, Jupi disappeared forever!

Elise Bell (10)
Lochside School, Dumfries

Alldawin And The Dragonborne

A long time ago, in a distant land, lived a beast called Alldawin. A man named The Dragonbourne called to the beast, 'Alldawin, come out, I demand!' Then the beast stepped out, he was giant, huge in fact, with horns as big as elephants, wings as big as mountains. His tail was the same as a rattlesnake's, his teeth were very sharp and he had as many legs as an ant. He had one big eye staring at The Dragonbourne, he could have killed him with one bite. But he wanted to be his friend, so they became friends forever.

Logan Byers (11)
Lochside School, Dumfries

The Sneaky Monster

One dark, stormy night in the city of New York lived a slimy, scary sewer monster, in the subway in a sewer. This sewer monster was the meanest monster in town and was known for causing trouble. After a while, the sewer monster left his lair and tiptoed into the city, wanting to cause trouble. He started throwing the trash everywhere until he saw his friend.
'What are you doing?'
The sewer monster was ashamed. 'Okay, I'll stop.'
Then they headed off to the sewer to have dinner.

Isla Talor Hammond (12)
Lochside School, Dumfries

The Homework Eater

Once upon a time there was a monster named Homework and he was from the train station. One day, he left and started to run to the bus stop to catch the bus and get to a school. He got on a really weird bus. After he got off the bus, he walked really slowly into a school. When he got in the school he ran to the classroom and hid in a cupboard. The children came in and he jumped out! He found their homework on the desk and he ate it all and he was sick!

Deryn Kathryn Wylie (11)
Lochside School, Dumfries

Sent Away

'Okay, I'll show you what powers I've got,' said Buddy Blast furiously. 'Mmm...' Suddenly, a big jet of colour came out his horn. Bright Band (Buddy Blast's older brother) and Buddy Blast stared open-mouthed!

'You're a disgrace! *Daaaad*!'

'What have you done now?' said Dad. 'You're going to Cloud Land *now*!'

Buddy Blast got to Cloud Land and a little Cloudkin came up to him and said, 'Name?'

'Buddy Blast.'

'Age?'

'12.'

'From?'

'Light Land.'

'Rainbow-making section on your first left, goodbye.'

When Buddy Blast got there he saw another firetip. He flew towards it and said, 'Hi!'

Eleanor Hemsley (9)
Pencaitland Primary School, Tranent

Untitled

Rex was trying out his newest invention when *boom!*
'Aargh!' Rex flew through the air at unimaginable speed. 'Ooof!' Rex crashed into a tree. 'Aww, my horn! That invention is going to the dump! Now where am I? Let's check my GPS, oh I must have broken it in the fall. My backpack is broken too.' At that same second he heard a shuffling from a bush. 'Hello? Who are you?'
'Zzzz.'
'Er, do you know English?'
'Zzzz.'
'Can you help me?'
'Zzzz.'
One hour later...
'A good old-fashioned slingshot. 1, 2, 3, go... Aaarrrggh!'

Noah Ellis Macdonald (9)
Pencaitland Primary School, Tranent

Flam And Squirt

Flam was just walking on his one leg when a little boy came by. 'Hi,' said Flam.

'Argh!' screamed the little boy and ran!

Flam used his hair to give himself a hug. A little while after, an elderly woman walked by.

'Hello,' said Flam.

'Don't eat me Mr Alien!' Slowly but surely she ran off!

Flam was lonely until another alien came. 'Hi,' said Flam.

'Hello,' said the other alien, 'I'm Squirt, do you want to look at my spaceship?'

'Sure,' replied Flam.

They walked and talked, then Flam and Squirt became best friends forever.

Ruby Mosses-Hoy (9)
Pencaitland Primary School, Tranent

The Feud

Snati and Bomb were best friends, yes they were best friends and when they were at school they were big pranksters. Bomb was hiding in the bathroom blowing up at people. Snati needed the bathroom. *Bang!* Snati ran out of the room, that was the end of the friendship. Bomb and Snati never spoke again.
Wait, it isn't finished yet!
Bomb started saying that Snati looked like a ship, so Snati got revenge. What Bomb didn't know was that Snati was a shape-shifter. Snati turned into a bomb and blew up!
They had a lifelong feud.

Zara Ashaye (9)
Pencaitland Primary School, Tranent

Spike

Spike awoke in the erupting volcano, he nearly fell into the lava! But Spike could hang upside down for ages.

Oh no! There was a baddy! He flew away with the baddy behind him. It didn't catch him.

After the chase, Spike went back to his shelter on Oompah-Loompah Land. He went to bed because he was so tired after the chase and escape from the erupting volcano. He slept for hours.

After his long sleep he was hungry, so he got some popcorn, his favourite food. Then he went back to bed.

The next morning he died sadly.

Niamh McLean (9)
Pencaitland Primary School, Tranent

Run!

Fluffems was working at the park, he saw an empty box. Fluffems ran to it and fell in it! He got mailed to Australia!
When Fluffems opened the lid of the box he realised he wasn't in the park any more, he was in Australia! Someone walked up to Fluffems with a cage, Fluffems showed his fangs and bit the man! What was going to happen?
Fluffems ran for his life. Oh no, a box and a pen fell out of the sky. It was the box Fluffems was in! He took the pen and wrote 'Antarctica'. Fluffems went home!

Rosie Graham (9)
Pencaitland Primary School, Tranent

Spotty Dotty

Spotty Dotty was in Cloudville walking home from the shop, she found a penny. She got so excited that she just had to blow... *boom!* She fixed the jigsaw pieces of herself back together. After she fixed herself she ran home to show her mum. 'Wow, very good,' she said, 'you can spend it on what you want.'
Spotty Dotty ran to the pet shop, she might blow up again! She got a skribble (a scruffy dog), she looked after it and called it Odie! Odie loved her and Spotty Dotty loved Odie. A lovely pair!

Iona McLean (9)
Pencaitland Primary School, Tranent

Blob To Earth

Blob is a monster ten centimetres tall. He has eighteen eyes, six arms and three legs. Blob has a fear of seagulls.

Blob's on his BMX when a seagull swoops and picks him up. He closes his eyes then opens them to see giant humans. He decides to use his horn to ask for help. While he is waiting, a jar slams down over him! *Slam!* He starts moving, someone puts him on the table. 'Time for dinner!' says someone. The person leaves and a spaceship lands next to Blob, so he climbs into it and goes home.

Lucy Elizabeth McMillan (9)
Pencaitland Primary School, Tranent

Running Scared

One day, Roncinch was plodding in the park then he saw Nocoby, so he hid. Nocoby was Roncinch's worst enemy, he was always trying to bite people. Nocoby saw Roncinch! Roncinch ran as fast as he could, but Nocoby was too fast and he caught up and tried to take a bite out of Roncinch's leg. But Roncinch managed to avoid it. Then Roncinch used his brain and turned around and ran! He was going to escape, then Nocoby got his brain working. He threw a trash can at Roncinch, who dodged it and ran into his house.

Molly Budgen (9)

Pencaitland Primary School, Tranent

Jingle Slob

One day, Jingle Slob was trying to avoid the sun as he was walking in the park. He misjudged his step and suddenly... the sun trapped Jingle Slob! One bit of the sun was on one half of him, the other bit was on the other side, so he was trapped! Whenever he would move the sun would move with him. 'Argh!' shouted Jingle Slob as he tried again to escape.

Finally, the rain came and he ran home to the planet Crog. When he got there everyone welcomed him by giving him cake and popping balloons!

Niamh Cadzow (9)
Pencaitland Primary School, Tranent

Aeroplane Vs Jetpack Fluffy

One day, Jetpack Fluffy was testing out his new jetpack by doing loop-the-loops and flying backwards. When suddenly, a very big aeroplane crashed into Jetpack Fluffy! He fell down, down, down, *crash!* He landed in a garbage bin. He thought and thought, suddenly he remembered the nuke launcher that he had saved for this very moment... revenge!
He aimed, he shot, he hit! No more aeroplane! 'Hooray!' he cheered.
From that day on all the planes stayed far away, yes very far away!

Duncan McWilliam-Snow (9)
Pencaitland Primary School, Tranent

Crusher

Crusher's boat crashes onto an island. The only inhabitants of the island are crazy cats. He's scared of cats because he was bitten by one. He uses his special jumping to escape from the cats. He jumps over twenty cats. He jumps up into the trees and swings over the heads of the menacing cats. The cats get mad but Crusher keeps on swinging. They hiss and try to claw him. Crusher keeps swinging and jumping. Faster he swings and manages to jump onto a passing ship to safety.

Elliot Smith
Pencaitland Primary School, Tranent

146

The Crazy Monsters

One day, there was a big monster called Lexi. Lexi was a very hyper monster, but a friendly one. She was all alone, what could she do? Lexi decided to adopt a pet, a small cute pet, a pet that was a mermaid! The mermaid was short with five eyes, she liked swimming and flying away.
Lexi and the mermaid went to the park, the mermaid turned fluffy in the water. The water got even colder and the mermaid turned even fluffier. But Lexi and the mermaid stayed together forever.

Kayleigh Brunton (9)
Pencaitland Primary School, Tranent

Untitled

Bob can turn into a bloodsucking bat. He flies to a small village in Scotland. He finds a house and sneaks in and hides in a corner. He sees Sophie's mum and follows behind her. Bob pounces and sucks Sophie's mum's blood. Sophie hears the commotion and she runs into the kitchen and grabs a pan form the drawer. Returning to the living room, Sophie chases Bob with a pan. Bob spots an open window and flies quickly out, back to his home.

Josh Noble (10)
Pencaitland Primary School, Tranent

The Stinky, Sticky Pads

Trevor shot out a lava pool and jumped right into the trap of the water griffin. He tried to bite out with his razor-sharp teeth. He got out! The water griffin attacked him but Trevor fought back. Trevor fired a lava ball, *boom!* The griffin was injured! The griffin was lying on the ground in pain. Trevor knew this was his chance! He got past him and ran and jumped back into the lava pool.

Finally, he went home to Mars.

Ollie Armstrong (9)
Pencaitland Primary School, Tranent

BlackArrow Is Back!

'Wow, what a lovely day,' DarkShadow said, while walking along the path. She was on a trip in Strawberry forest. DarkShadow explored for a long time until she walked into her enemy BlackArrow! BlackArrow was mean.

DarkShadow said, 'Sorry,' but BlackArrow just said, 'You will get payback!'

The next week DarkShadow was walking to school. On the way she fell into a puddle and got pushed into a bush. DarkShadow thought, *Oh, that's weird*. She walked into school, she had a weird feeling that something suspicious was going to happen. BlackArrow came to splash juice on her, but DarkShadow disappeared!

Julia Zuziak (11)

Pumpherston And Uphall Station Community Primary School, Livingston

The Bigfoot Encounter

Cico was sprinting at the speed of a cheetah on his daily sprint. He heard a ferocious growl.
'*Bigfoooot!*' he shouted.
Cautiously, he approached it. Suddenly, he jumped and started using his judo skills. *Crash! Bang!* The Bigfoot roared so loud that Cico was deaf for a moment! Bigfoot struck back and Cico fell to the ground like a dead elephant. Although the enormous Bigfoot almost killed Cico, Cico kicked him right back in his face. The big, fat Bigfoot was absolutely stunned and ran away screaming like a baby. Cico thought, *Wow, I didn't expect that to happen today!*

Rory Mclean (11)
Pumpherston And Uphall Station Community Primary School, Livingston

The Beast That Saved Earth

One day, a monster named Krypto from the dimension time and space, landed on planet One One Seven, aka Earth.

Suddenly, Earth was under attack from aliens then their mothership started talking, it said, 'Hello puny Earthlings, we are Ifnoraptor from Mars.' Ifnoraptors were primal beasts with fire coming out their tails and backs.

Krypto thought to himself, *I should save Earth.* The Ifnoraptors attacked so Krypto used his three eyes to shoot lasers at them.

Five days later, the battle raged on. Krypto sneaked onto the mothership and found a self-destruct button. He pushed it...

Craig Cantley (11)

Pumpherston And Uphall Station Community Primary School, Livingston

Sid's Sticky Pads

Sid, the lonely colossal squid, was purple with yellow spots. He had one short leg and very sticky pads. Sid was so fed up he sprawled out over some coral, turning invisible.

Suddenly, the most beautiful, sparkling mermaid in the sea, Aqua, started picking some coral flowers. Sid sneezed and the mermaid swam away! Then Sid heard a scream, it was Aqua the mermaid!

'Oh no!' cried Sid. 'Pinchy crabs.' And with that, Sid started spinning his tentacles, knocking the crabs flying with his sticky pads!

'Thanks,' said Aqua, 'let's be BFFs.'

'Yay, let's,' said Sid.

Paigh-Florence Dearie (11)

Pumpherston And Uphall Station Community Primary School, Livingston

Blinda's Adventure

Blinda was a spotty, five-eyed monster who lived on the magical realm island.

One day, Blinda came across a space-like creature, this space creature was a creature never seen before.

'Oh, did you hurt yourself?' Blinda said in a nurse-like voice.

The creature whimpered in pain as Blinda picked him up and took him home to treat him.

'Here you go, do you feel better now?' Blinda asked.

As Blinda asked him, his eyes started turning black and all of a sudden he shot out fiery laser beams and hit Blinda right in the eyeball!

Donatella Fargnoli (11)

Pumpherston And Uphall Station Community Primary School, Livingston

Earthquake!

Rumble, rumble. Earthquake! *Crash! Boom! Shatter!* Parts of houses came crashing to the ground. 'Help!'
Oh no! Nova thought.
The rumbling stopped, he looked around and heard someone screaming so he turned around and grabbed someone from falling from a nearby building. Then he used his super strength to lift a boulder off a woman covered in dust and then zoomed off to save more people.
At the end of the day he saved so many people, they all wanted to thank him in a special way, so they got all their resources and made a ginormous pie!

Kadan Brennan (11)

Pumpherston And Uphall Station Community Primary School, Livingston

Ulga Adventures

'Look, a bright light,' said Mulga.

'It looks like a window,' said Gulga. 'Let's go in.'

Suddenly, there was a bang!

'What was that?' said Mulga. Then a big black shadow appeared.

'I think we should go,' said Mulga.

So Mulga and Gulga opened a huge white door and climbed up some furry stairs, all the way to the top. But when they got there they saw a tall woman with blonde hair. When the woman saw them, she got a fright and then threw Mulga down the stairs and put Gulga in the toilet! Then she walked away!

Hayden Carroll (11)

Pumpherston And Uphall Station Community Primary School, Livingston

Waffer's Great Escape

Waffer woke up once again in her room, wondering what the day would bring. She unclasped her wings and polished her horn. She headed out... there were sugards everywhere around the island.

All of a sudden, Chocolate the devilcorn appeared out of nowhere, with his white fangs and dastardly wings, circling the island. Soon enough, the pink grass turned black and the rainbows turned to flames. Everyone was screeching for help. Walls blocked the exit. They were built with mossy stone and iron bars. All the magic was gone! There was no way out, or was there...?

Lydia Purves (11)
Pumpherston And Uphall Station Community Primary School, Livingston

The Crazy Classroom Creature!

Smash! Boom! In came a rocket ship with an alien inside it. The alien had purple, slimy skin with long, slimy arms and huge hands with big, sharp nails, big, gruesome eyes and fearsome teeth.

He looked at the very large teacher and the huge kids and took a massive leap onto the drawers and ran on the walls around the gigantic room. Then he jumped on the teacher's desk. The teacher slowly grabbed a fly swatter... *whack!* He moved out the way and launched over onto a student's head. So the teacher swapped weapons and splatted the poor alien!

Jack Redmond (11)
Pumpherston And Uphall Station Community Primary School, Livingston

Sweetie And His Enemy!

Sweetie is a loving, caring person who loves to share his sweets with everyone no matter what, because he believes that everyone should be treated the same. Sweetie loves to be kind but there is one person who Sweetie despises, this is Donald Trump, he owns planet Dump. Trump is a horrible person because he tries to stop Sweetie being kind and helpful. Trump's master plan is to trick Sweetie into thinking that Trump is a nice person and he wants to apologise for his behaviour in the past. He will then bring Sweetie to his lair.
What will happen?

Louisa Black (11)

Pumpherston And Uphall Station Community Primary School, Livingston

Monster Of Almondell

Bubbly looked around himself. He didn't know where he was. He asked a human where he was, but all they did was laugh at him. He wondered was it because of his claws or fangs or crazy hair, or because of his bubbly body? He didn't know. All he knew was they were bullies.

He saw a sign that said *Almondell Country Park*. Bubbly thought to himself, *If humans think they can pick on me, I will scare them, all the humans that come into Almondell Country Park!*

So Bubbly did that very thing and scared all the humans away.

Lewis Patterson (11)

Pumpherston And Uphall Station Community Primary School, Livingston

The Terrifying Journey Through Floodland

Bang! Flame woke up in a strange land he'd never seen before. Escaping the pod, he reached for the window therefore he saw different colours and... water. Flame had to be extremely cautious because he knew water was very violent. He managed to land his pod perfectly on the side of the building, making it able to let Flame in the room with the frosted window. A door handle creaked as it turned. As quick as a flash, he hid under the bed. 'This is risky,' he whispered, peering outside. He ran as fast as his little legs could go...

Jack Ryan Taylor Hamilton (11)

Pumpherston And Uphall Station Community Primary School, Livingston

Splifer's Journey

Once, there was a creature called Splifer. Splifer was small but could still be seen by lots of creatures.

One day, Splifer saw a rocket plan so he copied the plan and off he went.

All of a sudden, the rocket broke! He landed on Planet Zelch. Suddenly, a grey door fell off the rocket. All of a sudden a sign popped in front saying *King Kuba Says Leave!*

Splifer saw a junkyard for rockets, so he went to get another rocket. Suddenly, King Kuba shot a rocket at where Splifer was standing. *Bang!*...

Matthew Rutherford (11)

Pumpherston And Uphall Station Community Primary School, Livingston

162

Blue Goes Grey

Far away on a distant planet there lived small, fluffy, cute blobs that were bright, beautiful colours. Blue was a young little blob, he was only ten years old and already knew what he wanted to be when he grew up. He wanted to be a happy spreader.

Ten years later, he was spreading happiness to his planet but one blob he was making happy was from Dull Land and before he knew it, *boom!* The dull blob shot him with a colour drainer and he was quickly turning grey. When he looked at himself he cried black tears.

Hannah Anderson (11)
Pumpherston And Uphall Station Community Primary School, Livingston

Planet Weird!

Hip, hop, Jaffawuffle went. 'Off I go with my friends to deliver some food,' he said, but then a hand grabbed him. He fought and fought and some time later he was free; he thought it was because of is superb fighting skills, but it was not.

He travelled on to find his friends. Then, out of nowhere, a weird little thing tried to grab him and then more came, he could hear shouts. Soon he was out and then a weird-looking animal chased him, and suddenly he found himself on planet Jaffeur.

'He's home!'

Shannon Vermeulen (11)

Pumpherston And Uphall Station Community Primary School, Livingston

The Quest To Find The Gloop

'Starrp!' Spotticle yelped as he launched himself through the entrance to the underground cave. He landed with a clunk when he fell through the entrance.

The cave was no ordinary cave, it was full of priceless gems!

As Spotticle turned, he saw a house in the distance outside the cave. He was curious and wanted to check it out.

When Spotticle arrived at the house he knocked on the door, no one answered. Spotticle was still curious so he entered. Inside, he saw weird things he had never seen before...

Ella Rachel Watson (11)

Pumpherston And Uphall Station Community Primary School, Livingston

The Special Dragon Egg

One day, there was a special dragon egg with flames on it and a different design on it to all the other dragon eggs.

When the dragon was born, little did the dragons know that their world was crumbling because the different dragon had been born, and the only way to stop it was for a green flame to hit the core of the Earth. Only one dragon was able to that, the different dragon.

The world would end in thirty years...

Twenty years later, the special dragon went on a tough journey to the core of the Earth...

Lewis Campbell (10)

Pumpherston And Uphall Station Community Primary School, Livingston

Tiny-Tim

One day, Tiny-Tim was playing when he saw Mister Bubbles. Tiny-Tim ran up and said, 'Hi, how are you?'
Bubbles pushed Tim away and said, 'Go away you furry freak!'
Tim got up and ran off. He got to his friend's house and told him everything. His friend asked if he wanted to watch a funny movie to cheer him up. So they laughed so much and at the end of the movie they had a sleepover. Tiny-Tim felt so much better but he still felt bad for Bubbles. But he was too tired to think.

Sophie Campbell (11)
Pumpherston And Uphall Station Community Primary School, Livingston

The Mystery Of The Missing Friends

One magical day, I bumped into this crazy creature called John. He was telling me all about himself. He was telling me that he came from Mars and that he was really good at maths, but he needed glasses to read and then he started introducing me to all his friends. They were really nice people. Suddenly... an earthquake happened! We all fell to the ground. We didn't know what was happening, so then John got up and was looking around for his friends, but he couldn't see anyone. He didn't know what to do...

Kimber Shearer (11)
Pumpherston And Uphall Station Community Primary School, Livingston

The Monster

One day, a little monster went outside and played. She used her wings to win games and stood up pretending to be human every day. Her mum said, 'One day we will go to Earth, I promise.'
The monster looked at the Earth and said, 'I'll try to go there.'
After three years, she flapped her pink wings and flew there as fast as she could. When she got there she could not believe it. She looked at the sparkly blue water and green fluffy grass. She looked around and saw a tall thing...

Samantha Price (11)

Pumpherston And Uphall Station Community Primary School, Livingston

The World That's Underwater...

Seama rushed across the water, hoping to meet new friends. In Seama's spare time she made clothes from her wool and had a lot of friends that were like her. But then while she was swimming she found a group of sharks and they weren't happy, so she tried to use her wool but it was all soaking wet so she used her wings to fly, but then there were birds after her! So she used her clever instincts to become invisible and left the sharks in a state of bewilderment, and she was never seen again.

Sophie Martin (11)

Pumpherston And Uphall Station Community Primary School, Livingston

Monster From Mars

One sunny day in the city, a black cloud came over and a monster fell down from the sky. He had six legs, Cyclops' eyes and suddenly disappeared! Then he tapped me on the back and took me away to a secret lair, strapped me to a chair and left me so he could get more people!

But my friends helped me escape, and the FBI and police came to help us destroy the monster. We all got a monster kit and tried to eliminate the monster. Finally, we did it!

Cameron Brydon (11)

Pumpherston And Uphall Station Community Primary School, Livingston

Ogzy The Big, Lonely Giant

In the mountains of Russia lived a big, lonely giant called Ogzy. He lived in a small cave all alone because everyone was scared of him.
He had big wings, two strong horns and fangs. Ogzy could breathe fire. No one visited him because he smelt like a one-thousand-year-old egg. Ogzy liked the cold, he was a predator, but wasn't at the top of the food chain.
Ogzy wanted to change his life and have friends.

Aaron John Cleland (11)

Pumpherston And Uphall Station Community Primary School, Livingston

Pablo's Peril

Pablo is a bright blue laser-eyed alien. He comes from the Planet Alienlandia.
One day, Pablo entered a spooky cave where no one had ever returned from. He got halfway through and suddenly realised he was lost. Then he saw a light ahead.
'Am I free?' said Pablo.
Then he recognised it was actually an animal hunting for aliens.
'Oh no, looks like it's the end of me forever!'

Katie Martin (11)
Pumpherston And Uphall Station Community Primary School, Livingston

Galumph And Mia!

One beautiful morning, in a lovely village, lived a freaky monster in a small hole. It was very cramped. Galumph, the monster, might seem hostile on the outside but he is actually kind and caring but everybody hated him.

One day a warm-hearted girl called Mia approached Galumph and said blissfully, 'Would you like a better place to live?'

Galumph replied, 'Yes please kind Miss.' Mia was delighted so she took him home and explained how misunderstood he was and that he was kind and loving. He knew he could call his new place his lovely warm home.

Sophie Elizabeth Childs (10)

Ranworth Square Primary School, Liverpool

Untitled

One foggy day a crazy monster was walking through the streets, scaring people. The monster had always crept at night, hurting and scaring people.

One day the old, poor people were working away. A few minutes later the young, bad monster came back and frightened everybody.

The monster went out again that night, frightening everybody but in a different way. Soon a scientist asked the people about the crazy, young monster. 'Why did the exotic monster attack you?'

'Well, a monster one day came to town and freaked out everybody.' But that monster was gone.

Sophia Shaw (7)
Ranworth Square Primary School, Liverpool

The Meanie Monster

Legend has it a long time ago lived a meanie monster. He was a huge monster who lived in the forest. One winter's night a little boy called Coby was snatched in the forest. 'Help!' he shouted. 'Help! Help!'
'Just the boy I needed,' the monster shouted. 'You are not getting released until you do what I say.' So Coby got the wood for the fire, he even ate what the monster ate. Suddenly it all came to an end. Coby said, 'I've had enough.' And he stormed off. The monster woke up and realised he was all alone.

Ella Dambis (10)
Ranworth Square Primary School, Liverpool

Michael And The Monster

One day Michael was playing with his cars in his garden. He heard a thudding and a squeaking noise. Michael stood up, looking into the trees. He was scared, looked towards his house; when he looked back his car was gone. He saw a massive footprint where his car had been! He felt brave and followed the footprints. Michael froze in horror, he saw a massive, green haired monster with the biggest hands ever! He had large googly eyes, when he smiled he had odd shaped teeth and he smelt of cheese. His nose was an elephant's trunk that squeaked!

Samuel Scott Mercer (8)
Ranworth Square Primary School, Liverpool

A Simple Potion

Daydream lived inside a pitch-black cave, next to a gorgeous river. He'd never been out of his cave because he feared that the people who surrounded his home would be scared of him.

One day, he had a great thought: he'd make a potion and pass it to all the feared creatures of the land to make them normal. He would finally go out into the gloomy world he had feared for so long and gather herbs for his potion.

His great claws met the muddy ground for the first time. He turned his head to look. *Bang!* He fell.

Lexi McGreevy (10)

Ranworth Square Primary School, Liverpool

The Long Tooth Green Monster From Mars

There's a monster who sleeps in the day and wakes at night. There was a human walking past this creepy, old, falling down cottage in the woods. He stretched out his mouth and snapped for the human and got him.

The walking wind was blowing the cottage down bit by bit. The monster did not like it, he was angry. He was following a local family from round that area but they did not know, the kids were saying they'd seen a monster but the adults just ignored them. Suddenly the monster snatched the kids; the adults should have listened.

Adam Dean (11)
Ranworth Square Primary School, Liverpool

The Fly

A fly got into a lab. The scientist saw it and rolled up some paper to hit it. He couldn't but he did hit test tubes. *Smash!* All the substances mixed together, the scientist ran. With a big explosion like a volcano it covered the fly.
The fly realised he was different. He was bigger, very clever and could move things with his mind. The scientist returned, the fly hid behind the door. The fly got his own back when he made the scientist roll up some paper and hit himself with it. All the other scientists laughed.

Harry McMahon (10)
Ranworth Square Primary School, Liverpool

The Mad Mouth Mini Monster Of Mexico

Adam Opeqe was a kind man, he lived in Mexico with his family. He always went for nice walks, rain or shine. Little did he know, on the far edges of Mexico there lived the Mad Mouth Mini Monster of Mexico, the very monster Adam would come face to face with...

Adam had wandered into a dark cave, the only source of light being the sun. Behind a sharp rock there was a mini growl. It was Mexico's Mad Mouth Mini Monster! Adam accused it of being a pink bear cub. Adam took a trip to sudden death as punishment.

Ellen McNulty (10)
Ranworth Square Primary School, Liverpool

Attack Of The Kyba

On a normal day a girl called Olivia was sitting by a tree with her pet cat, Bella. On that day she went missing, her parents were searching for days. Meanwhile, while Olivia was gone the Kyba captured her. The Kyba stays in a cave. On that day Olivia realised that she had a tracker to track her down but by that time the Kyba struck. She was lying there still. The Kyba was sitting there on top of Olivia, then out of the blue a magical creature appeared, a yellow Chocobow. He shook his hair and attacked the Kyba.

Taighlor Rogerson (10)
Ranworth Square Primary School, Liverpool

Elliot

Once there was a monster called Elliot and he loved going on crazy adventures! Once he jumped off a bridge! Crazy!

He wanted to discover volcanoes so he jumped out of a helicopter into the volcano but then he realised that he couldn't breathe because lava is as hot as the sun. He wasn't prepared so he started to worry and couldn't stop.

So he thought if he flapped his arms it would work. So he tried and it worked! He landed gently and was happy so he lived happily ever after.

Leah Sephton (8)
Ranworth Square Primary School, Liverpool

The Crazy Monster

One stormy, wet morning me and my family were all fast asleep in our warm beds when suddenly we were awoken by a really loud noise. We all didn't know what it was. So we looked all around the rooms, up and down the stairs and in the garden. We still couldn't find anything. Then we heard the noise *again*. It was coming from upstairs. We all ran back up the stairs and into the bedroom to see what was making the terrible noise and wow, a slimy, crazy green-eyed monster!

Nathan Boyle (7)
Ranworth Square Primary School, Liverpool

The Two Tone Creature From The Sewer

Slugger from the sewer ate people from office buildings, cars and houses. He was not a nice creature. He stretched out his tentacles and wrapped them around people's waists and then ate them. As Slugger went to eat more people another, bigger monster crashed through the window of an office building and hit Slugger with his huge feet then ate Slugger all in one piece.

Luke Lawless (7)
Ranworth Square Primary School, Liverpool

Revenge!

Coffeemocha, a 17ft tall, coffee coloured, scaly monster was floating in the desert. One day, drinking a sweatachino he met his arch-enemy Tealeaf gliding towards him. Coffeemocha yelped and threw his drink at him and floated off swiftly. Unhappily Tealeaf thought about where Coffeemocha had gone because he wanted to throw a tea bag at him for revenge.

Later, Tealeaf finally found Coffeemocha at the sweat vending machine buying a sweatachino. He throws the tea bag at Coffeemocha with such force that it knocks over Coffeemocha's drink into a bin. 'Bullseye!' shouts Tealeaf, gliding off to the desert.

Max Marnell (8)
St Alban's Catholic Primary School, Wallasey

Braincrush At The Rescue!

Once there was a monster called Braincrusher. He lived in Anthenna Land with lots of fierce creatures. Braincrusher was lonely and had to do jobs. The others picked on him because he was peculiar. Braincrusher could see the world with one eye. Flashbaze and Machine Creature were good at keeping Anthenna safe from humans. Braincrusher could see in the far away distance, a bright saucer in the sky. It was moving quickly, it was humans! Braincrusher told Flashbaze and Machine Creature that they were in danger. Braincrusher destroyed the saucer using radiation from his magnificent eye! He saved Anthenna Land.

Ebony Michelle Johnstone (8)
St Alban's Catholic Primary School, Wallasey

Goultar Saves The Day

Goultar and his friends were playing monster tag. Suddenly, Insidious appeared on Goultar's planet Venus. Insidious had no friends because he was mean to everybody. He played evil tricks on everyone. Insidious hated recycling and so he mixed Goultar's and his friend's recycling waste with non-recycling waste. Goultar was determined to find him as he was ruining his beautiful planet. Insidious liked gold so Goultar decided to encourage him to go to Mars where there was plenty of gold. So Goultar told the Martians about Insidious and they threw him in a dungeon. Goultar became king of his planet.

Marco Clenkian (8)
St Alban's Catholic Primary School, Wallasey

How Shelly Belly Got An Enemy Called Jellnastics

Shelly Belly had been living on Mars for three years and was on her way to live on Earth but halfway through the journey another creature called Jellnastics came on the plane. Jellnastics really likes to do lots of gymnastics; Shelly Belly thinks it's silly.

'Wahoo, we've landed on Earth! Jellnastics, have you ever been to Earth?'

'No, why would I? Can you please stop sitting down and go outside because I've heard Earth is a nice place.'

'Why is Jellnastics so mean and bossy?' Jellnastics and Shelly Belly became worst enemies ever.

Ellie Toner (8)
St Alban's Catholic Primary School, Wallasey

Crazy Creatures

Slobers was slouching down the pathway, he had no home to go to. He suddenly saw a snake-like bath, it expanded into a gigantic slimy snake pool. He saw Blanbi, his astonishing enemy. He hated him.

'I'm sorry, let's teleport to Lapland,' said Bonker.

'Who are you?' said Slobers.

'Oh sorry to just come into your friendly conversation,' said Bonker.

'We are not friends,' said Blanbi.

One second later they were in Lapland. Slobers and Blanbi were amazed, they became friends over the awesome experience they had been through.

Chloe Mary Kathleen Hammond (8)
St Alban's Catholic Primary School, Wallasey

The Fall Of Cybertron

There is a transformer called Death and he transforms into a dragon that shoots fireballs at his enemies, Megatron and Starscreen. He lives on Cybertron which is his home but the Deseptasons are taking over half of the planet.

Death escapes from Cybertron to Blurk which has Mushroom Island and he transforms into a dragon and shoots fireballs at the mushrooms and they roast mushrooms. Then King Mushroom comes and Death has to shoot a mega fireball to destroy the mushroom king's army. Mushroom Island vanishes in a blaze of fireballs.

Ozz Kindred (9)
St Alban's Catholic Primary School, Wallasey

Skaran And The Volcano Battle!

Deep in a volcano below the Hawaiian Islands, Skaran, a dragon shark, was swimming in the bubbling lava. He bumped into his arch-enemies Pyro-Shark and Lava-Crab. Lava-Crab pinched Skaran but Skaran blasted him with his fire-breath and killed him. Next, Pyro-Shark chased Skaran to his home and showered him with meteors. At the same time Skaran summoned his fireballs. They crashed violently together, making a sonic explosion, knocking Pyro-Shark to the bottom of the volcano, never to be seen again. Skaran was repelled rapidly back to his home where he had a boiling fire shower.

Reuben Spivey (7)
St Alban's Catholic Primary School, Wallasey

Transilvan's Victory!

Transilvan strode along on his three felt feet. It was a gloomy night and Transilvan heard a dripping of a pipe, then appeared Dr Strange and Black-Eyed Pete. Transilvan then shot six lasers and fired at them but they got back at him so he was knocked down. It was tough now so Transilvan used his super strength on them but it still didn't work! Eventually he used his unicorn horn powers and blasted them to weakness. Dr Strange and Black-Eyed Pete died and everyone that lived on Neptune was happy now that they had won and adored Transilvan forever.

Eva Easdown (8)
St Alban's Catholic Primary School, Wallasey

The Big Battle Is Now!

Danger was strolling around town very peacefully when suddenly he heard a loud *bang!* He turned and saw millions of robots. The Instructor must have sent them! They were using gunpowder to blow up roads. *Crash! Bang! Kaboom!* Danger had to stop them and protect the city. Danger knew he had to act fast to stop Instructor. Danger began a storm, lightning bolts came down from the sky crashing into the robots, breaking them into tiny pieces. Danger was running like a lion to catch up with Instructor. He caught him and put a stop to the evil Instructor.

Alfie John Feeney (8)
St Alban's Catholic Primary School, Wallasey

Battle Against The Richest Dragon

Midnight Dragon set out to discover the lair of the richest dragon. The rich dragon heard of this quest and dispatched his henchmen to stop him. The wolfpack intercepted Midnight Dragon on the mountainside. The battle was intense; only the dragon's laser beams were enough to defeat the wolfpack.

After the wolves a phoenix went to battle the dragon in the mines, just before the lair of the rich dragon. This time Midnight Dragon had to transform into a lava robot to win. Face to face with the rich dragon Midnight discovered he was old so he became the richest.

Chloe Ashley Blyth (7)
St Alban's Catholic Primary School, Wallasey

The Spitting Sparkle Queen

One day the Spitting Sparkle Queen spat on her husband, he became a monster like her. They keep control with their powers but the next day their powers were going out of control. Her husband, Spitting Mike, had rainbows shooting out of his bum. They had to move back to Planet Smelly Feet because they were on Mars. They put on suits so their powers wouldn't go off, but it never worked. They set off, Queen Spit Sparkle was spitting, turning everyone into monsters. The humans were running for their lives but they weren't fast enough. Everyone was a monster!

Libby Hamilton (9)
St Alban's Catholic Primary School, Wallasey

Killer Tom's Dreadful Adventures!

Killer Tom was always hungry, in fact his favourite food was hot dogs but Killer Tom had eaten all the hot dogs in Monster Land. He was told to go to Wales, so off he went. He was thinking how many hot dogs there were, but could only find real dogs so ate all the dogs, except one. The dog said, 'Don't eat me,' with a growling woof. 'I know a better food.'

'But what food could be better than delicious hot dogs?' said Tom.

'Well,' said the dog, 'my favourite food is cat.'

So off Killer Tom went. Yum-yum.

Eleanor Claire Cronin (8)
St Alban's Catholic Primary School, Wallasey

Who Will Be King Of Two Planets?

Bloodshot was an ultimate teleporting, six-handed, lumpy magician. He loved being prince of Planet Guts and kept watch with his eight googly eyes. Dingbat and Hooded-Claw wanted to kidnap him and feed him to the Minotaur. There was an epic battle! Bloodshot used his shape-shifting skills to become a big mouth dragon. He singed off their hairy, spotty noses with one yeti roar, which made all his eyes glow in the dark! Dingbat and Hooded-Claw ran as fast as their sticky pads could go. They had lost the battle and Bloodshot was now Imperial King of two planets.

Harry Jonathan Smith (8)
St Alban's Catholic Primary School, Wallasey

Fireblast Stops Crafty Crab5

One day Fireblast was gliding to a beach in Hawaii called Colocucu to meet his friends for their monthly campfire. Usually Fireblast made the fire with his fire skills. They toasted marshmallows on the campfire. There was a mean crab called Crab5. On that day while Fireblast and his friends were eating toasted marshmallows, Crab5 purposefully put the campfire out and he wickedly stole the marshmallows. Then Fireblast became invisible, crept up on Crab5 and flipped him over. After that, Crab5 said to Fireblast, 'I will get you one day Fireblast!'

Sam Funcks (8)
St Alban's Catholic Primary School, Wallasey

Beauty And The Owl

One day a creature called Beautymaid was playing with her mermaid friends in the Candy Land Ocean. Beautymaid looked up and saw her mysterious enemy, Mystery Owl. Then, she leaped out of the water as fast as lightning. The water flew up with a giant *splash!* Mystery Owl was flying in circles trying to confuse Beautymaid but it didn't work. So Beautymaid shape-shifted into a very scary monster. Mystery Owl was scared. After Beautymaid asked Mystery Owl if they could be friends, she said yes. So off they went playing a game of tag in the sky.

Harry Marshall-Hose (8)
St Alban's Catholic Primary School, Wallasey

Botland

This is Fuzzbot, 'Haha,' he says all of the time. 'I am a really, really big age. I am nine.' Fuzzbot has a fuzzy belly and wibbly wobbly funny legs. He is a Cyclops because he only has one eye. Fuzzbot's best friends are called Timbot and Tombot, they're funny. Fuzzbot lives in a little small village called Botland, he is the most unique bot because he has fuzzy hair unlike all the other bots who are metal and shiny. He is in a football team and it is called Funky Footballs, it's the best team in his village.

Sophie Baker (8)
St Alban's Catholic Primary School, Wallasey

Splobby Gets Chased

There was a monster who lived near water, his name was Splobby. He had an enemy, a nasty monster called Bone Crusher. Splobby was exploring near a cave, he went inside and saw Bone Crusher, he was terrified. He was a super fast runner so ran towards his home. When Bone Crusher came out of the cave he saw footprints. He smelt the footprints and knew it was Splobby. Bone Crusher followed the footprints to Splobby's house. He chased Splobby but Splobby was too fast and jumped into some water. Bone Crusher could not swim so he went back home.

Woody Clewlow (8)

St Alban's Catholic Primary School, Wallasey

The Sneaker Stasher

The first time I realised we had a monster living in our house it was the school holidays, me and my brother were playing hide-and-seek, looking for a hiding place. I thought it was good to hide under the floorboards. I opened the crack in my bedroom floor and let in air so I could breathe through the little hole. I crept in and discovered that Stasher was there hiding too. He had arms and legs that expanded and a tongue things could stick to. My brother didn't find me. I stayed with Stasher till Mum shouted me for dinner.

Ashton Traynor (8)
St Alban's Catholic Primary School, Wallasey

Decsie's Christmas

Decsie the monster is round with one eye. He lives up the chimney where he hibernates until the first of December when the Goodwill family put up their Christmas tree. Decsie can make himself look like a bauble. He likes to watch the family. Tilly the cat knows Decsie is alive and tries to chase him.

One day, when the Goodwill family were in bed, Tilly chased Decsie around the house. Then Santa came down the chimney and scared Tilly off. 'It's OK Decsie.' And he puts Decsie on top of the tree where Tilly can't get him.

Amy Goodwill (8)
St Alban's Catholic Primary School, Wallasey

Plonk Vs Plonkytan!

Plonk walked to the elgy shop in Gar Gar Land. He saw a new shop and went in. Waiting inside was Plonkyton waiting for him. Then he attacked Plonk. He was stronger than Plonk, Plonk hit him but it didn't hurt Plonkyton so he used the bottom of his feet to stab Plonkyton. Then Plonk fell over. So Plonk pushed Plonkyton over so he couldn't get back up but he did and Plonk hit Plonkyton and beat him. Plonk then continued to shop and got a digit gun to protect himself. Then Plonk got home and fell asleep quietly.

Reuben Swaine (8)
St Alban's Catholic Primary School, Wallasey

Sandstorm's Battle

It was a cold and frosty morning when Sandstorm woke up in his giant bed. He opened his window and there stood Zetro Mexar. 'Zetro, my enemy, I will get you,' said Sandstorm. Sandstorm had to think fast. Suddenly Sandstorm flew out of his window so fast. He went to help the other monsters in danger. He was about to strike when he found all the Zots surrounding him. So he opened his mouth and blew out an enormous sandstorm which sent the Zots flying to the ground. Then he blasted Zetro into space and he was never seen again.

Orla Maguire (8)
St Alban's Catholic Primary School, Wallasey

The Invasion

One dull day in a green and white school Lexy, Ollie and Petra were having a maths test. They got told off for not doing their work and looking out of the window instead. Then they saw something land in the playground. An alien crawled out of the spacecraft. Everyone screamed but Ollie laughed. Ollie had seen this alien before, it was called Fire Bong from the planet Extraverganser. Ollie remembered it was afraid of mice. Ollie told his friends, they ran to the science lab and let out the mice. The mice scared the alien away.

Isobel Prescott (9)
St Alban's Catholic Primary School, Wallasey

One Floofy Bobble Hat

In the Victorian era, as the first bobble hat was placed in a glass box to be safe for the night a scientist broke in and stole the hat and electrocuted it. But what? It seemed to come alive! 'I'll call you Floofy,' he smiled, but it broke out of his grip and Floofy lives to this day. Last week Floofy heard a small girl crying and saw she had been forced to draw a massive picture with many crayons. Floofy threw himself in the bucket of crayons and ate the lot, then burped in the teacher's face. Payback!

Sadie Pearson (9)

St Alban's Catholic Primary School, Wallasey

Creatures

One day there was a creature called Hanky-Doodle and he had an enemy called The Googly-Eyed Monster. They had a fight but made friends, then they had a fight again and they always pick on each other. But one day they had a real fight. There was a village nearby but they didn't know who to believe because they always tell lies so Hanky-Doodle did the spinning kick and The Googly-Eyed Monster had a bruised eye. They made friends and played tag together and Hanky-Doodle promised never to do the spinning kick again.

Rio Emerick Grant (8)
St Alban's Catholic Primary School, Wallasey

The Magical Story Of Egger The Egg

One morning, Egger and Egger's little sister, Eggy, were walking on Planet Egg when they fell off Egg Land and landed on Crayon Land. While they were exploring Crayon Land, King Crayon and Queen Crayon found two eggs and drew all over them then ran off laughing. Eggy asked Egger what to do and Egger told her to break herself and the crayon would be gone. Then the two eggs broke themselves and were all normal. The two eggs ran back to Egg Land, then King Crayon came back to find that the two eggs had run home.

Lucy Louise Donegan-Bowen (8)
St Alban's Catholic Primary School, Wallasey

Spooky Sam Returns

Freaky Frankie is a creature of the underworld. He has laser beams that shoot from his top three, wet, sticky eyeball antennas and flies super fast with ginormous fluffy ears.
One day he bumped into Spooky Sam, his biggest enemy. He had a Cyclops eye and could shape-shift into different monsters. Suddenly Spooky Sam shape-shifted into a yeti and roared really loud. The roar hurt Frankie's fluffy ears so he couldn't fly. Frankie used his lasers to scare Spooky Sam away. The underworld was safe again.

Sammy Michael Sheldon (7)

St Alban's Catholic Primary School, Wallasey

Crazy Doo's Magic Spaceship

One day Crazy Doo had a box of magic spaceships that could take you to any destination in one second. He wanted to go to Earth. Suddenly Lucky Boo's master told Lucky Boo to destroy Crazy Doo's spaceship. Lucky Boo broke the spaceship with his sword. Crazy Doo got out his magic tools and fixed his spaceship. The only way to scare his enemies away was to do a back flip and boo really loud. 'Boo!' They ran away to their base. Crazy Doo went back to Mars in his spaceship and is at home.

Christopher James Mannings (8)
St Alban's Catholic Primary School, Wallasey

The Sock Monster Who Turns Evil

There was a monster and he was tidying up a boy's bedroom and he touched a stinky sock. Then *bang!* He turned into a sock monster and he became evil. He went crazy and started to cut up every sock he could see. He went mental. He tried to eat the boy because he was wearing socks. He ate the boy's mum and then he bit off his mum's neck because she would not let him eat the mum's socks. And then he ate the whole house. He was very angry because they would not let him eat their socks.

Chloe Louise Williams (9)
St Alban's Catholic Primary School, Wallasey

Untitled

Googlie is the protector of Peanut Island with five eyes and wherever she goes she knows what other monsters want to do to her. She can look in every direction and she can fly. She has no enemies because she is loved by all monsters. It's Googlie's birthday so her friends have thrown a party. Peanut jelly and peanut butter butties and a peanut butter birthday cake. Here comes Googlie. 'Happy birthday!' they all shouted.
Googlie was surprised, 'Let's party,' she said.

Romilly Carol McKinnon (8)
St Alban's Catholic Primary School, Wallasey

Bloop's Adventure

Bloop was a friendly little alien exploring the solar system when his fuel ran out and he crash landed on Earth. Bloop was having a look around when he saw a flying creature, he thought it was Rusher, a highly dangerous creature. It was only a normal bird though. Bloop used his shape-shifting powers to hide. After the bird had gone he went away and in the distance he saw another alien. He rushed over and asked, 'Do you want to be friends?'
A year later they had an alien family underground.

Finley Connor (9)
St Alban's Catholic Primary School, Wallasey

The Boggle Monster's New Best Friend

Bob went to Earth, trying to make some new friends because he didn't have many friends in Boggle Lands. At first people didn't like him as he was a giant monster, but after a couple of days some of the people started to like Bob because they saw he was friendly and pretty. When it was time to go his new friends invited him back anytime he wanted to go back. Bob was happy with his new friends and arrived back in Boggle Lands smiling from ear to ear. He couldn't wait to see them again.

Kaitlyn Olivia Lomas (8)

St Alban's Catholic Primary School, Wallasey

Jef The Fish

One day there was an animal called Jef. He lived in the river Mersey. Jef hates school, he saw a school and heard all the noisy children. He blew fat bubbles and spat water at the children and the school. He met loads of famous fish like Dory and Nemo. He can also fly and get out of the water. Him and Bill the eagle are best friends. They're always playing tag. There was just one enemy, the shark in the water. Every time the shark saw Jef he bit the fish but Bill pierced the mean shark.

Joel Henri-Reid (8)
St Alban's Catholic Primary School, Wallasey

Torchu's Adventure

Torchu went for a walk down a path. It was very quiet until he heard a strange noise coming towards him. He decided to hide behind a bush which is quite hard as he is a big orange creature with four long legs and two huge yellow wings. As he stomped behind the bush he fell down a hole, the noise got nearer. Torchu was shaking until he realised the noise was his friend Squirt Mander, a blue turtle with a long tail which has fire coming out of it. He turned it off to help Torchu out the hole.

Luke George Howells (8)
St Alban's Catholic Primary School, Wallasey

The Space-Douglar

One day a fantastic thing happened to me, I was on Mars, staring at the fabulous Milky Way. Then suddenly I saw a scary alien on the Milky Way. It told me its name was Ronald and it said, 'I'm scared of creatures from Earth.' I advised him that he shouldn't be scared. But then all of a sudden he was surrounded by, well, aliens. I came to the rescue and saved him just before the space bullies could do anything to him. After that the aliens were no longer scared of humans.

Oliver Timson (8)
St Alban's Catholic Primary School, Wallasey

The Adventure Of Sawman

Sawman has come from the Hell Dimension; raised by the Devil. One day the Devil sent Sawman to Earth to destroy humans. He was causing mayhem in the city until a tank shot him down. He got put in prison, but they forgot to take his saws off him so he escaped. The president made a deal that he wouldn't cause mayhem and he could stay so he went back all the way to Hell, tried his best to destroy the Devil and won. He was in a bad way so came back to Earth and lived happily ever after.

Joseph Hesketh (8)
St Alban's Catholic Primary School, Wallasey

Bad Choice Of A Pet

One day it was foggy and the doorbell rang. It was a pet owner to give him a pet cat. Once he came home from school he found his room in a mess. The monster was fluffy and spotty. He tried to stroke it, it was warm but fierce. Henry ran quickly towards his lab. He grabbed an empty bottle and some ingredients: grass, banana skin, bacon and watery milk. Henry put them together as quickly as he could. He felt like he got trapped in the house by himself. He poured it quickly, it worked!

Charlotte McNeill-Williams (8)
St Alban's Catholic Primary School, Wallasey

Untitled

Once upon a time there was an alien called Clive and he lived on a planet called Zarzar Planet. Zarzar had a population of 11,000 aliens so Clive was not alone.

One day Clive was having breakfast, he turned on the TV and it said that Planet Zarzar was going to be attacked so he started to feel sorry for Planet Zarzar. He made a speech and from that day they had shared countries and learned to never judge anyone for their looks and they all lived happily ever after.

Mai Allen-Coates (8)

St Alban's Catholic Primary School, Wallasey

Crazy Dan's Life

Once upon a time there was a monster called Crazy Dan, this is his life. One day he fell into a deep portal and ended up in a forest so he explored it.

One hour after exploring he became BFFs with a human girl. They met an old woman and he ate an apple off her. After the apple Crazy Dan turned into a vampire, he was still BBFs with the girl.

Two hours later Crazy Dan turned back into a monster and he enjoyed life and lived happily ever after.

Gracie Bird (7)
St Alban's Catholic Primary School, Wallasey

Chocus' Spell

Once upon a time there was a place called the Secret Forest and a person called Chocus who was a magical turquoise fox with magical powers. He could open the doors of the houses with his eyes and whack people with his long fluffy tail. But one day he forgot the spell to open the doors, he felt miserable so he sent a message using his mind to his friend's town and that town gave him a book so he re-learnt the spell.

Adam Williamson (8)
St Alban's Catholic Primary School, Wallasey

Frank From Mars

Frank had four eyes and he lived on Mars. He was stuck on Pluto and he didn't know how to get home! He walked for ages and found some old meteor and built it into a rocket. Then he realised he had nothing to power it with so he walked for a bit and he came across some rocket fuel. Then he took it to the rocket and flew home.

John James Howard (9)
St Alban's Catholic Primary School, Wallasey

Fire Hazard's Found Enemy

One day a creature was walking through the forest and he found his enemy, his name is Ice Cube. When they found each other they had a huge fight. Now they're best friends and they both save the whole, entire world with some help from other superheroes they meet on their journey. They now even have their own superhero league.

Charlie Curtis (8)

St Alban's Catholic Primary School, Wallasey

Untitled

On a cold winter's night Icebod was creeping around in the deep, dark night. Joseph heard many stories of Icebod and his pet Icenam. He didn't believe he would ever come and take his teddy. Joseph ran the tap to see if the noise would make Icebod come. Icebod climbed through the window, he was half asleep. Icenam came out from under the bed; he took Joseph and Icebod took his teddy. His mum and dad didn't hear it.
In the morning, Joseph's parents looked everywhere for him. They called the police but he was never seen again.

Maddison Grayson (9)
St Helens PACE, St. Helens

Kitty And Bush

In the icy night, Kitty lurked in the shadows, waiting for people to vacate their tents. Mr Bush was disguised as a raspberry bush to protect the people.
Suddenly people came out of the big blue tent. Kitty was bouncing from tree to tree. A man was right under the tree, he was the perfect target. Kitty slid down the tree, Mr Bush pushed her out the way. It was time for Mr Bush to end this once and for all. He chased her through the fields, releasing his thorny arms, ready to finally defeat Kitty.

Larissa Wood (10)
St Helens PACE, St. Helens

Untitled

Human Trap was an invisible monster. He lives in Liverpool, sometimes a picture of him appears and he looks like a Venus fly trap because he has no legs. But when he is invisible he has legs. Today he set off to London and when he got there he saw a little girl, turned invisible and walked up to her and gobbled her up in one big bite.

Next he saw a chicken and ate his tall feathers and then all the pets chased him back to Liverpool.

Emilie Kelly (7)
St Helens PACE, St. Helens

Untitled

Gift is a lazy, stupid weirdo with two bums. He wants to win a medal for being the greatest monster. Gift is supposed to catch mice with all the other monsters and Gift tries but this makes him sad. Not today. He pounces, he has got it! An enormous, furry mouse! Proudly he plops the mouse in front of the chief monster, Gift is now the proud owner of the greatest monster medal. He happily shows it off to all his friends.

Sharyn Billingsley (7)
St Helens PACE, St. Helens

Untitled

Foxy is an alien, he can make never ending candy. Foxy comes down from Mars in his spaceship to give me and my friends some never ending candy. But Snatch is waiting and comes to take Foxy. I save him, I tie Snatch down, keep his eyes open and make him watch Frozen, the worst movie ever. Whilst Snatch was screaming in pain we said, 'That's what you get.' And we enjoyed all the candy.

McKenzie Briers (7)
St Helens PACE, St. Helens

Princess McMuffin

Today Princess McMuffin is a pink muffin and princess of Candy Land. Her favourite wrapper dress is yellow with diamonds.

She was lonely in scrumptious Candy Land, so with her magic she created friends, doughnuts and cupcakes. She was thrilled but something was missing, she needed love. She ventured to her basement for ingredients but toxic food colouring turned her green! Doctors then made her pink. Although her appearance was great, she still felt something was missing.

After many failed attempts, Princess McMuffin finally baked her perfect prince and they lived together in the warmth of Waffle Palace.

Tara Divito (10)
St John's Primary School, Edinburgh

Killer Carrot

Evil Carrot Man is a blood-covered carrot with an orange cape and messy hair. He goes around killing people with amazing hair. Or he tries to, at least. Pizza Man, his nemesis, distracts him till they have stopped eating.

One dark and dingy day, PM and his friend, Cakedude, came to EMC's lair. Cakedude was an award-winning food barber, so he offered to do EMC's hair.

Of course he said yes, and in five minutes he declared, 'Thanks, dude. Actually, I'm going to change my name to Kevin the Carrot!' They all laughed and lived together as best friends.

Mia Morrison (10)
St John's Primary School, Edinburgh

Charninja

Charninja is one deadly dragon creature, with ninja equipment and powers such as its sword that's sharp enough to chop a building in half, and it has a flamethrower which is over 300 degrees Celsius. One day the Postman was doing his job when, all of a sudden, Shuriken went flying past him and he got in a van, but everywhere he went he found he couldn't escape. A dragon ninja appeared in his face and cut him with his sword, and then burned him.

People say that whoever sees Charninja never see their family and friends again, so beware.

Imran Mohammad Zafar (10)
St John's Primary School, Edinburgh

Brainshifter

There is a deadly creature called Brainshifter who has a huge brain and can shape-shift. He is allergic to water and has his own cave.

One day, a couple who were on their honeymoon came across his cave. The male said he wanted to explore, the female said she'd wait for him outside. She heard a blood-curdling scream then she called the police.

When the police were exploring the cave for evidence, they came across twenty-one bodies! They saw a man with blood on him, at least they thought so, because he had stabbed everyone with his hand!

Finlay McWilliam
St John's Primary School, Edinburgh

Hammer Head

There was once a hammer called Hammer Head who has a home but no friends. He likes eating metal and fat people and loves hammers. Hammer Head gets stronger every year and gets one metre bigger every year. Worst of all is he gets angrier every year and destroys everything. He gets whatever he wants. He eats metal things like big machines.

Then he eats every person and thing in the world, then he meets a metal tool called Screwy. Screwy beats Hammer Head, and since, Hammer Head eats everything. Screwy is the only thing alive for ever and ever.

Danny Lewis
St John's Primary School, Edinburgh

Deadly Doughnut's Story

There was a doughnut called Deadly Doughnut. He was bullied a lot. Every time he was bullied he would get angrier and angrier. Deadly Doughnut had no friends, he was alone.

Now one day he was so angry he created his own friends, they were deadly dangerous monsters but something went wrong. Monsters he made put something on him, it was toxic. The toxic made Deadly Doughnut turn into a monster, he had blood eyes and fire powers. After he killed his mother he turned normal again and nice, he forgave the bullies and his friends were never seen again.

Himmat Singh
St John's Primary School, Edinburgh

Ghostly Ghoul

When darkness falls, a ghost blows with the wind going in houses of intelligent children.
The ghostly ghoul is stupid; he breaks into houses of smart children and sucks their blood to get as smart as J.K Rowling.
One day he was looking for the perfect child to kill, suddenly he sensed a nine-year-old studying Algebra. He went in but no one was in.
Ghostly Ghoul was creeping around houses, he couldn't understand, there were no children. He had no energy, he was going back to the grave. He was screaming, he fell to the ground lifeless, dead.

Motiya Muzzamil (10)
St John's Primary School, Edinburgh

The Chewy Pencil Chewer

Mandy Lockhart had opened the door to find the cutest teddy ever. She picked the toy up and gave it a hug. It turned into its true form, The Chewy Pencil Chewer.

It took a humongous bite into her head, blood dripping down her face. The creature spotted her school bag, rummaged around and found her pencil case. Never had this purple and pink monster ever seen so many scrumptious pencils. *What a feast I will have tonight*, he thought.

With three juicy pencils stuffed in his mouth, it saw Mum. What was he going to do? He must hide!

Freya Auchincloss
St John's Primary School, Edinburgh

The Scary Story Of Scares

In a forest not so far away lurks a scary monster with two heads, teeth that can go through anything, two tails with spiked clubs, poisonous claws, death staring eyes and black body.
This is known as the Scary Scarer of Absolute Scariness lurking in a forest.
One day it saw a black something on the floor, it was chasing him and he never lost it. And that night in that forest was so scary because of it. He nearly died. He was unconscious for months. When he regained his full consciousness he realised... it was his shadow all along.

James Craig (10)
St John's Primary School, Edinburgh

Monster Town

In a town called Monster Town there lives a monster called Olly.

He is a bright, colourful monster with an incredible tongue, three and a half eyes, and he of course loves to burp. He has loads of patterns on him. He was online and he saw an advert about a competition. It was a competition about how long your tongue was, so he went down to the long tongue competition. They measured Olly's tongue, it was 24ft long.

He eventually got the results and was the winner. He never thought he would win, he was so surprised.

Emily McKenzie
St John's Primary School, Edinburgh

The Jealousy Of King Blob

King Blob was very angry because his gran would not give him more cake. 'No, you are too fat,' said his gran.

One day, King Blob felt really annoyed with himself, so he searched for the fittest person he could find. He found Cristiano Ronaldo.

The next day he went to a gym where Ronaldo was training. Ronaldo was running, then he saw him.

He screamed like a girl, then he ran. King Blob was very happy because Ronaldo won't be fit much longer after seeing King Blob.

Last I heard Ronaldo lived in a cave, never seen again...

Fred Davis
St John's Primary School, Edinburgh

Blamos

Blamos are pill-looking monsters. They came out of a pill box, they have wings and shoes. Amazing, fascinating, eye-catching, weird, cute creatures! The Blamos danced around crazily and had loads of fun playing football. They played catch and frisbee and played in the sink and the toilet! They played the Xbox. They had loads of fun playing around the house but the old man was coming back! So they had to go back into the pill box now. But just before, they went to the kitchen and ate the crackers! They went back now but they had fun!

Beth Adams
St John's Primary School, Edinburgh

Revenge Of The Cacti

One day, a scientist was trying to create a power source from cacti but something went wrong with the experiment and the cacti came to life. The scientist kept the cacti, the two baby cacti were called Chiara and Conor, and the two adults were called Catie and Cody. Cody had a prickle gun, prickle machine gun and prickle rocket shooter with lots and lots of prickles.

One day, Cody found out that the scientist was going to kill them and afterwards dissect them, so Cody and his family enslaved humankind and ruled the world.

India Faith Young (10)
St John's Primary School, Edinburgh

King Stretch Face's Story

There once lived a creature called King Stretch Face who could, if he wanted, change into anything he wished to.
King Stretch Face found his power when he was working as a dentist; he accidently swallowed a numb jag so whenever he spits he spits numbness. One day he turned into a monster and made sure nobody could see him then he went up into Edinburgh to look for people to eat their brains, but for the first time, he spat on somebody but it didn't numb their body so he took their brain. The person felt it and died.

Lewis Johnston
St John's Primary School, Edinburgh

The Weird Story

There lives a creature so scary no one believes it's possible. It never blinks and has a chainsaw mouth and it can grow and it can shrink.

When someone comes, he shoots three of his kids out of his chainsaw mouth. When people walk by he can also shrink.

One time someone caught Red Eye and got a photo, but he swallowed him whole and ate the camera into 101 bits.

Back at home, which is a ball with an eyeball picture on it, someone shoots him but that isn't the end of him.

Sean Brannen
St John's Primary School, Edinburgh

Captain Crazy

One day, Captain Crazy who does crazy things was doing something crazy, he was going to jump of the highest tower in the world *ever!* He came out of his hideout, the crazy cave, and made his way to the crazy car and started driving to the tower. On his way he saw a cliff by the beach and decided to jump off it. He climbed it and jumped off. When he got there he was asked if he wanted a parachute but he said no. He broke every bone in his body and still survived.

Liam Murray (10)
St John's Primary School, Edinburgh

The Elf On The Shelf

There's an elf, looking for a job. He's tried 200 places.

'You're too mischievous,' they would say. He's at last found a job at Pizza Casa. He's being very good so far, because no one's annoyed him, but he's got one chance. He's been tempted, once or twice. They've been watching him.

But one day he got fired! He stormed off in anger. He wanted revenge. He came back in disguise and bought a pizza and smacked it in their face.

Splat! All over their face! 'Hooray!' he shouted.

Noah Jackson (8)
St Saviour's Catholic Primary School, Ellesmere Port

Madness Of Monsters

Batiza has all the amazing tricks, he turns into a mermaid at night and can turn his eyes red, when he's scared fire will start coming out. His friend Fluffy Fangs has invisible problems; he can always make himself invisible. Batiza and Fluffy are BFFs, everyone says so. It was night, Batiza wanted to play hide-and-seek but he couldn't, he was a mermaid. They didn't know what to do so as the sun rose they played hide-and-seek in the forest.

Clancy Lillia Oldam (7)
St Saviour's Catholic Primary School, Ellesmere Port

Fnaf Horrors

In the morning the Animatronics gathered round and had a peaceful breakfast. When they had finished they would go backstage to practise their jumpscares. When Foxy practised his jumpscare everyone could hear him in the pizzeria. After that they'd perform to the kids, Bonnie, Chica and Freddy would sing songs but Foxy was different. He would stay in Pirate's Cove. He's not allowed to leave Pirate's Cove.

Amber-Alexis MacDonald (7)
St Saviour's Catholic Primary School, Ellesmere Port

The Crazy Creature Scary Story

Once Puffer Power was a crazy creature and appeared in water. When it's night Puffer Power comes to you and steals your homework and eats it up like a beast. He then comes to your classroom and eats up your other homework. Then he gets a sword out and starts cutting open more boxes of homework and gobbles the lot of them. Finally he goes back to the sea until the next night.

Katie Jones (7)
St Saviour's Catholic Primary School, Ellesmere Port

YoungWriters
Est.1991

YOUNG WRITERS INFORMATION

We hope you have enjoyed reading this book – and that you will continue to in the coming years.

If you're a young writer who enjoys reading and creative writing, or the parent of an enthusiastic poet or story writer, do visit our website **www.youngwriters.co.uk**. Here you will find free competitions, workshops and games, as well as recommended reads, a poetry glossary and our blog.

If you would like to order further copies of this book, or any of our other titles, then please give us a call or visit **www.youngwriters.co.uk**:

Young Writers
Remus House
Coltsfoot Drive
Peterborough
PE2 9BF
(01733) 890066
info@youngwriters.co.uk